WAYGATE

Charlie Nash

Published in 2020 by Flying Nun Publications, http://flyingnunpublications.com/

ISBN:
978-1-925775-25-9 (ebook)
978-1-925775-26-6 (print)

This project is supported by the Queensland Government through Arts Queensland.

A catalogue record for this book is available from the National Library of Australia

Cover design by Richard Priestley

About the author

Charlie Nash was born in England and holds degrees in mechanical and space engineering, medicine, and writing. Her fiction has been shortlisted multiple times for the Aurealis and Ditmar awards (and she is fine with being the bridesmaid). She lives physically on the eastern seaboard of Australia, and mentally in any number of parallel storyworlds.

 charlienash.net
f authorcharlienash

Also by Charlie Nash

SHIP'S DOCTOR STORIES

"The Ship's Doctor", *ASIM* #47 – 2010

"Dellinger", *Use Only As Directed* – 2014 (Peggy Bright Books)

COLLECTIONS

Men and Machines I: space operas and special ops

Men and Machines II: punks and postapocalypticans

All Your Dark Faces

SHORT STORIES

"Deep Deck 9", *Luna Station Quarterly* #10 – 2012

"The Edge", *Scareship* #8 – 2012

"Jack", *Mysterical-E* – Fall/Winter 2012/2013

"Parvaz", *Dreaming of Djinn* – 2013 (Ticonderoga Publications)

"Tartarus", *Electric Spec*, Volume 8, Issue 2 – 2013

"The Message", *Dimension6* #1 – 2014

"Blue ICE", *ASIM* #59 – 2014

"The Ghost of Hephaestus", *Phantazein* – 2014 (FableCroft)

"Alchemy and Ice", *ASIM* #61 – 2015

"The Seven-forty from Paraburdoo", *The Never Never Land* – 2015 (CSFG)

FLASH FICTION

"The Two Boys", *Every Day Fiction*, 3 July 2011

"Migration", *The Journal of Microliterature*, 22 January 2013

"The One You Feed", *One Page: Brisbane*, 20 January 2014

"The Lady with the Lantern", *Pseudopod* Episode 428, 6 March 2015

"The Last Gate is the First", 2018 BWF UQ Microfic comp longlist

ALL AT CHARLIENASH.NET/STORIES

Author's note

Waygate is technically the third tale in the adventures of the ship's doctor, but it is the first of more substantial length (the other two are short stories) and can be read alone. If you'd prefer to read the saga in order, however, this print edition includes the first two stories as a bonus at the end. Flip over to page 73 if you would prefer to begin at the beginning.

—Charlie, September 2020

1

This is the way things go on approach to a waygate. About two clocks before, an unbalanced energy touches everyone on the ship, as if the human engine is about to blow a rotor. Pretty right, I suppose. If you really sat down to think about a waygate, about how it shreds a ship into data clicks and hurls it across stars and vacuum and into another place, you'd have to be silicon-based not to unbalance about it.

We're two clocks out from the waygate now. I've been standing by the forward viewing port, watching the pinprick star of it growing brighter, contemplating the jump through all that black space, and what's on the other side. Warm smells occasionally drift down the hall from the galley deeper in the ship, but the spices aren't familiar. Nothing to pull a memory, anyway.

Two clocks to go. That's fifty hours before Riley and I can make the first of three jumps back to the Jupiter Gate, and be on that last leg to Earth. I feel more than just the two-clock jitters this time. It's the pressure of what's behind us, pushing, reminding. We've left the *Dellinger* and the *Freya* behind, physically. But the traces of those episodes have laid down sparking wires in my memory, and its no use trying to pull them out.

The only answer is to run.

Riley would say that was stupid. And I'm inclined to agree, in that sensible, insightful part of my mind that has little control over what I actually do and say. I've been running since the day I left the inner circle systems. Slowly, carefully, all the way to the outer edge where there was nowhere left to go. And now I'm on the way back in, a comet that reached apogee, commanded by orbital dynamics. For a time, at the turnaround after the *Freya*, I felt a settling. But maybe that was just turning a corner, backward momentum cancelling out the forward for a time. And now that the waygate is growing in the forward port, from a shining speck in the blackness to an actual shape, I think I'm all forward momentum again, bound fast for anywhere but here.

I'm still staring at the gate when Riley finds me.

When's the last time you jumped this gate? he says into my mind.

I shrug, though I know exactly. A month before I landed on the *Freya*. It took two jumps through waygates and then snail-time on a transporter to get all the way out there. I plotted the course myself. There's people who'll do that for you – optimize the transit time, or the cost, depending on your criteria – but I've never used one of them. If I wanted to, I could put my hand to this transport's comms line and pull a course plot from the ship's central algorithms. I feel my fingers open, anticipating me doing just that, but I stop. Lately, bad things happen whenever I use the neural graft. The last one was to advertise my presence on board a transport liner, which attracted a parasite ship looking for someone like me. Real happy adventure, that one. Got out alive, but not without dragging up cold-store memories that I came out here to forget.

So I ball my fist inside my pocket, and shake my head instead, closing myself down to Riley talking into my brain.

But his question is still there. When's the last time?

I wonder if he's asking because his homeworld, the Voyager system, is on the other side of that gate. A first-order system, which means areas of dense civilization. At least three developed planets, and as many moons, orbiting stations and space-object processing platforms. A good number of lesser-known secretive bases, too, but we've both been avoiding thinking of such things, replacing them with ideas of orbiter tea houses and farmstay food stops. Riley came from somewhere within all of that. He hasn't talked about it, but anticipation's been building in him about this jump, more than the last one, and that time we were harboring fugitives. We left them at a tech reconditioner in the system behind us, and booked this private transport with a crew of two who keep well to themselves. But Riley's tension has been growing. Or maybe it's just that, for once, I've been paying more attention to him than the ship we're on.

The time has brought a new closeness between us, that I've naturally been resisting like old tempered steel. I'm good at resisting. I roll potential replies to his question around my head, words that would ask him about the last time he jumped this gate, or the last time he saw his homeworld, something normal that would follow his lead.

Only I don't say them. Instead, I watch until the growing star of the waygate splits into two, and I'm relieved there is something else to say.

"What is that?" Riley says.

"There's something else out there. As big as the waygate."

I came through this waygate on the way out to the *Freya*, and it was a solo station then. One lonely gate out here in the black, the more far-flung end of its pair, the other side back in Voyager. Voyager itself has five gates, maybe more by now. First-order systems have many. But this system didn't last I was here. Another star-like speck can only be a few things: a blue-class mega-station, like the *Freya*; a massive interstellar freighter; or another waygate. A blue-class would only be in planetary orbit, and a freighter would be in a shipping lane for the gate, which it clearly isn't. So, this can only be another waygate.

"You think that's a blind river?" Riley asks, because he's decided that it's another gate, too. Would bet he saw it before I did, with those grafted eyes of his.

I don't answer as we stare at it. A blind river is a waygate that's breaking new frontier out into the 'verse. The far end would have been built maybe twenty circles back in central-time — close enough to twenty Earth-years — strapped to a set of fusion drives and pushed out on a long sail. Bound for a distant system that some enforcer-guarded think-tank had scheduled for a new fingernail hold of humanity in the blackness.

The near end … well, that's what we'd be looking at. Newer technology than its mate, who'd already been sailing for decades across the vacuum. That's the way it works out here — the further out you go, the deeper back in technological time.

And while I need to drag Riley back to the bunk sometime in the next half-hour, that new waygate out there is unnerving.

"You hear anything about a new waygate coming online?" I ask, because I've been avoiding news feeds, too. I don't want to hear about what system governments have held elections, or promised to have them, or been taken over by a junta. Or the latest projections for shortages of various ores in which systems. Or ads for reconditioners, food recyclers, job agents, or recruitment lines for interstellar service.

Riley doesn't answer me, and I'm about to repeat the question when I notice a fine vibration coursing through his mind. It's like nothing I've ever felt before, not even in a ship. I touch his arm, and there's a tremor running through his skin, too.

In that tremor is memory and emotion, excitation and fear, all twisted together in an Escherian loop. It feels engineered into him, some kind of warning system.

What? I say. We both carry secrets, but they are not normally the kind that boil under our skin. They're the kind we keep under lock and key, that we don't even speak to each other in the space-dark bunk.

Bad feeling, he says. Which in a man whose Special-Ops training probably aimed to excise *feeling*, is doubly a reason to move.

Something's not right. There's another ship out there. Enemy ship.

He moves to the corner of the viewing room, then the other, peering into the space outside. Rigid. I can imagine him in battle fatigues. I put my hand to the bulkhead then, looking for reassurance from the ship. It takes a run of seconds to tune in, longer than it normally does, which is odd, as though this ship speaks a language I haven't translated in a long time. But finally, I tap in, and the communications begin spooling into my mind.

I frown.

There's almost nothing going on. The kind of quiet you expect in a transporter running through vacuum on a long haul. No beacons, no message relays, no alerts, no flags at all.

Riley pauses his sweep to look at me, and I look back at him, into those red-rimmed grafted irises. Him so full of feeling, me so devoid of it.

Too quiet, I say. Too quiet for a transport approaching a waygate, which normally buzzes with the pre-authorization checks, manifest certifications, clock synchronizations, and all the other data-work that using a sensitive technology requires. Solar hell, this is the kind of quiet that's trying not to be noticed.

I push my senses further, flicking through data channels, looking for what I'm missing. I'm risking betraying myself, but something isn't right here, and right at the heart of the ship, I sense an odd configuration about it, as if her data lines were run to an alien protocol. I pull my hand back with a bad feeling, too. We missed something here.

And then, as though our thoughts have manifested action, I hear the air moving in the hall. Two heartbeats later and there's three bodies in the doorway. Two of them are the crew we've seen before, but there's a third in front, wearing what I think is a dull green suit. But my eyes keep sliding off the side of it, and then my vision swims, just as I see a glint of metal in those hands.

❬❮❯❭

I short out for a minute. It's not a blackout – I'm dimly aware the whole time of moving through the pressed ceramic hallways of the transport, of the dull green suits around me, the smell of their plastic fiber fabric, its weave leaking molecules of the bodies underneath – but my mind just won't run right. There's a binding pressure around my head, and I'll just be getting to the boot-point of full consciousness, as if I'm waking from sleep, and something derails and I fall back under. I've maybe done this six times when we reach the bunk. I know where we are because I can smell Riley here, that smooth machine oil and cinnamon of him, mixed with the synthetic flower scent on the sheets.

Movement stops. Voices. I reach boot-point again. This time, there's a yield feeling, a tension that frays loose inside my skull. Whatever broke allows me to come awake. But I know it's not all of me.

"Consciousness, but five ticks late," says a cold feminine voice, like a ship reading a status. My hands fly up to my head. There's a snug, helmet-like thing over my hair, strapped with a metal clip under my jaw. It hums with an unpleasant energy. I can feel that energy pressing down on the part of me that didn't wake.

"Longer times to consciousness are expected when brain grafts are offline," says another voice.

Then I understand. They've put a neural disruptor on me, so that I'm back to how I was before I was a ship's doctor. Just the brain I was born with. It feels like flying an unfamiliar shuttle with the flaps shot out, all ungainly on the controls.

But that also means ...

They know who I am.

That thought comes with a black tar sickness. I can almost smell the bad news among all the smells in this cabin and on these bodies. As if I've caught the shakes Riley had looking out at the waygate. This isn't a robbery. These aren't coup leaders like the ones on the *Freya*. They've come here for me.

When I can remember how to form words, and the room is back to a blurry gray square, I try to look at these three crew. The one in the front – the one with the cold ship's voice – I still can't keep my eyes on, and I realize now that it's because of her suit – some kind of disruptive pattern that sends my depth perception wild whenever she moves. I've never seen anything like it. I have to keep my eyes above their heads, where I count them by height: One, Two, Three. Or move my gaze to their feet, which are covered in thin toe-shoes, the kind that people wear to be silent running on ship decks. And as I watch, Two and Three, the crew we've seen before, touch their collars and their suits shift into the same disruptive pattern as the one in front. That's some high-end gear.

I say, "Are you military? Or pirates?"

They don't answer. In fact, despite the heft of their bodies and their superior gear, they keep an oddly respectful distance. Finally, Two stabs twice at their handheld screen as if checking off my status. I can imagine what's on that list. *Conscious*, check. *Forming syntactically coherent sentences*, check. A bit ordered for pirates, so I'm betting military. I have a moment's fear, that these are contractors sent to bring me back to where I started, but it all this seems too unfamiliar for that. The screen goes in a pocket.

"We have a full clock until the jump," the one I call One says, in her flat accent. "You'll remain in bunk until then. You'll be briefed on the other side."

"What about the agitator?" says Two, meaning Riley, who is somewhere beyond my left elbow.

"As he was. We want this smooth and by the count."

One leans down then, near enough that I can smell a curious mix of skin oils and laundering spray, the signature of long-term shipside living. She has long eyelashes and a sharp haircut, but soft skin over her cheekbones. Definitely female, probably a career militant. Carefully controlled and by the count. Maybe that's the distaste I feel in her gaze; career militant animosity for non-militants. I wonder if she's about to speak threats, but she only adjusts the neural disruptor, and the strap squeezes skin against my jawbone.

She grunts and steps back, and Two and Three pull out of the door. It closes, but I suspect at least one of them will remain outside. My hands go straight to the disruptor, but it's a cage around my head. My arms fall back, powerless. I look at Riley then, at the bruise already seeping purple across his jaw.

"We got some trouble," he says, pressing a palm to his temple. "Some real awful trouble."

I look out into the inky expanse. I can't see the gates from this porthole, but they're out there: two stars growing brighter in the darkness.

"They're going to jump us," I say.

Then I look at Riley, and I can see in those red modded irises that he knows these people don't mean to jump us back to Voyager. These guys are going for the blind river. They're going to jump us out into uncharted space, and to whatever's waiting out there at the end of the ride.

2

The throbbing in my head eases as a full clock ticks over, and it comes with a sense of slipping away from myself. They bring us hot food passed through the door hatch, but I don't eat it. I've a horrible sense of loss for that part of my brain that I never really wanted to begin with. A burden I've carried for decades that now I can't not carry. Life is all threaded ironies.

Normally, I would have been able to reach out to the hull of this ship, follow the vibrations until I came close enough to a comms line to tap in, and poke around to find out what I wanted to know. Like, who the fuck are these people? And where in the chain of my existence did I crosslink into theirs?

But this disrupter around my skull has muted that channel. All I can do is sit on the edge of the bunk and run thoughts over and over. Riley is quiet, and I have moments where I wonder how much damage they did to him, and whether whatever implants he has left from Special Ops are running restoration now. But it's a thought I don't seem to be able to hold on to. The only question I don't have to ask is *what do they want*, because that's apparent, and I don't want to get to the *why* just yet.

"*Coryn.*"

I stop. My name on Riley's tongue always feels foreign. It's clear he's said it more than once now.

"I said, did you notice their suits?"

"Disruptive pattern," I say, but I'm the one who feels disrupted. "No logos, names or serials."

"I have a feeling …" Riley says, as if he's trying to drag the bottom of his turbulent memories for the one that's relevant here. "An old feeling. Do you know who they are?"

I shake my head, which strains my neck muscles with its unaccustomed weight, but something is definitely weird. More off than just being hijacked right before a waygate. I push myself up and stumble around the bunk. If they've muted my ship-sense, I'll have to go old-fashioned, and rely on my eyes and ears and nose.

This ship certainly looks like a garden-variety private transport. Middle of the line. Molded panels of gray recycled polymer. Air-filled bunk mattress. Piped recycled water. I pump some into a cup and taste it. Clean. Really clean. Better than expected for a transport we boarded on a remote system moon.

I frown, and pace around on the bunk floor. The disruptor is throwing out my balance, but I could swear the grav-deck in this ship is better than normal, too. Low quality ones often have microwobbles in the gravity field that induce a low-level nausea, but I haven't noticed that once since we came on board. The only time I ever remember better were on inner-system, high-end transports. Most of the outer systems still don't have that quality of grav-deck, and when I saw this ship in the dock before we boarded, it looked like an ordinary, mid-sized outer system transport.

So, something isn't right.

"Help me," I say to Riley, trying to pry a side panel off the bathroom wall. It won't come loose, so we try another, and eventually, we lift up the mattress to peer down into the store space below. A smell hits me then, a clean bright chemical, like the burst of a meteor across the sky. It lights up an old memory, loaded down with warning flags.

That's when I see the edge of a double panel. All the gray recycled polymer? It's been stuck on top of the real fabric of this craft. I run my finger over the smooth edge of an aerated xerogel panel. That material is the lightest, strongest, most expensive stuff in the 'verse. I smelled it in the development labs, back when I was in training, before I was made into what I am. A memory that survived the process. So these aren't pirates or some regional military. They are something else.

It's Riley who snaps his head up. I can almost see the plug ends of his memory connecting together. He makes a gesture of warding off evil that's pulled from some deep cultural history. Something I don't know about him, long before he was Special

Ops and had those eyes. Something he learned from a caremother, or a grandmother, or someone else who gave a shit whether he lived or died.

"Kraysis," he hisses.

I feel my eyebrows shoot spacewards. "Kraysis?"

It's not a name I would have expected. No one talks much about the Kraysis. It's not like they're a secret, it's just they're not tied to Earth-central anymore. They were part of a second-order colonial expansion, the first system to be colonized not from Earth, but from another system. It was called the K-system, then, over five-hundred circles ago, and many who settled there would never have seen Earth. So it's maybe not surprising there was always a tension between them and the Earth-central, one that resulted in them opting out of the trade connections that bound everyone else to the mother planet. "Opted out" was the term histories used, but records about it are slim. They only say the Kraysis took possession of their waygate and shut it down, and that was all anyone knew of them for most of the last five-hundred circles. Information just can't cross light-decades of interstellar space without a waygate. I remember a line in the histories about an atrocity related to the gate closure, but it had the abstraction of long ago when the colonial expansion was still in early days. A lot of madness went on. They were just the crazy K-system.

Rumors pop up, of course. Legends of espionage and raids the Kraysis still visit on Earth-central systems. About as reputable as stories told to children, about half-dead men who live under their bunks. I used to not put much stock in those legends.

Only now, looking at Riley's face, the way he's throwing open all the hold spaces searching for his gear, I think those histories might be slim for a reason. And I think of the *Dellinger*, which was also supposed to be a legend, and how I knew different. How that legend could just come out of black space and make itself real.

"Everything's gone," Riley says, stepping back with his fists opening and closing. If I could touch inside his mind right now, I'm sure I'd see Kraysis memories running in his neural circuits. I wonder if in Riley's past position, he'd have reason to know more about the Kraysis, because he's gone as pale as the xerogel wall.

"What do you know about them?" I ask.

He pauses before he says, "You know how you've heard they're just like us? Well, they're not. They're the most dangerous thing in the 'verse."

"Then why would they wait? If they were going to take us, why not do it when we first came on board?"

Riley looks around the cabin. He shrugs. "Maybe they would have, but we were less trouble when we kept ourselves in here. They didn't take us until you started reading their ship."

He's right about that.

And now, they have us.

We start to feel the pre-jump bounces then, the weird ripples the waygate makes on approach to its portal. Someone once told me, way back before I was what I am, that waygate jitters feel like waves bursting on the hull of an old sea-going craft. Not a large ship, like the ones that hold cities on ocean-bound moons, but the small ones old Earthers would push off some beach. Without positioning or maps or anything but some scrap of a sail, and a will to go from this point to somewhere else ... to leave a familiar shore for another. Across water they couldn't drink, but from which had come all the life we knew about. That same water would slap into a hull no bigger than an escape pod, pulled and pushed by a moon that for thousands of years, was the only one that people had ever seen. It struck me then how primal it must be to get on a ship and go without knowing the end.

Now, I feel a ripple of weird, remembering that conversation. A sudden wanting for Earth, a place I've never been. It's the same odd stirring I had when Riley and I first agreed to head there together. A memory pulled from someone before myself. It's unpleasant, like anything you remember so long after forgetting. Maybe it's the waygate dredging up these things. I've never jumped through one with the new part of my mind offline.

I curl into the corner of the bunk, tucking up my knees.

Riley sits on the other side, head bowed. "What do you think's at the end of the jump?" he says.

My vision is glitching with stars. I look around the bunk, at the lie of this Kraysis craft. Just a few hours ago, for the first time in my life, I'd had a sense of the tide running with us going to Earth. Back to the center of all the things, as if we'd find some answers there. Both of us on the cusp of talking about the things we'll say to no one else.

Now instead, we're about to be dragged through space against all that momentum.

"Something we're going to regret," I say, then close my eyes and turn away.

3

Here's what I see as soon as we make the jump.

The light changes, a noticeable shifting down the spectrum from the cold white of the previous system's star to a warm IR red. The red that glows in fire coals, one step away from burning to black. Wherever we've jumped to, it's a system with an old, massive star.

Out the porthole, at first there's nothing but space, but then we feel the jolt of a course-correction burn, and the disc of a pale blue gas planet slides in view. Riley jerks when he sees it, the instinctive reaction of a pilot to a large gravity object in the near field. He might even have implanted grav sensors, though we've never discussed it. Either way, a waygate is never placed this close to a planet. That's one of the unbendable rules of waygates. Despite the politics across the 'verse systems, all waygates fall under Earth-central command. That way, they can run on Earth clock standard, and be traffic managed, and be placed in optimized positions for transfer to other places. Important when it's days or weeks in transit between gates. Those are the public reasons.

So just looking at how this gate has spat us out in a near-planet orbit, I somehow know it wasn't put here by Earth-central.

"We're in a descent trajectory," Riley says, staring out the porthole, a hard edge in his voice.

My stomach dips. I think of dreams I've had, of falling forever down through an atmosphere to a massive planet that has no surface, the air glowing hot outside the window, waiting to burn up. "Descent to where?"

He gives a slight shrug, one that's containing an urge to break things. "There's another gravity blip out there. Smaller one. A moon I guess."

"A moon."

There's no announcement of the descent over ship comms.

And without that other part of my brain, I can't even tap the ship's data feeds as we spool down toward some unknown landing point. It's an unnerving, blind experience, and when the touchdown finally comes – a sick deceleration with a jolt and a vibration – I jump like a new recruit on their first trip out. I have to pick apart each sound to make sense of it, to feel anything like myself. The jolt was the landers hitting a rocky surface. The vibration is the thrusting engines winding down, maybe some contribution from surface dust aspiration. A slight tang comes into the bunk air, the smell of air passing over hot metal, which is from the reflection of engine heat off the surface.

Riley stares out the port hole, but his head is angled up now, towards something above us. I slip in beside him and follow his gaze. High up, just visible at the top of the port, is the red-lit line of a crater edge. The rest of the wall is all hard black shadow, but one thing is certain: we've landed in a deep chasm.

I have a horrible sense of impending revelation, just moments before that air rush comes back down the hall. Riley tenses, but when the door slides open, it's One and Two again, this time empty handed.

"The Developer sees you now," says One.

"Who?" I ask, just before Riley says, "The hell they will," and steps in front of me.

One stares at Riley, as if registering his presence for the first time. Her expression turns curious for a click, before it dims to disregard. I can almost hear her thoughts – assessing what threat he represents, and rapidly arriving at near zero. The confidence of a militaristic technological culture, who are holding the keys to the only way back across the 'verse.

Riley knows it too, and he must still have his Special Ops pride, because he hates his odds. I can feel his animosity even without him talking into my head. But there's animosity in me for him, too, for the way he's behaving. These Kraysis are obviously well organized militarists, so it's just balling stupid to lean on those inclinations. I know he's smarter than that.

I take one slow breath, shift the weight of the neural disruptor, and move around him.

"Coryn, *don't.*"

And do what instead? I can't speak into his mind, but my poison look is enough. Chastised, his red grafted irises shrink, but his mouth compresses, too. Rebellious. He's dangerous like this. The kind of recruit they threw out the door on the first day.

"Stay here," I tell him, not kindly, as I follow One out of the door.

❰❬❭❱

One leads the way to the forward viewing port, where Two and Three stand outside its door. I'm expecting some kind of inquisition beyond, but there's a single figure with his back to me, standing in the same place I was when the Kraysis first came for us.

I can tell, from the care and reverence of One, Two and Three, that this is *the Developer*, but he's nothing like I expect. Where the other Kraysis are thick-limbed and broad-chested, the Developer's sharp shoulder blades make ridges in the back of his suit, which is less than half the width of One's. His hair is fine and pale. He's tall but with a hunched neck, his overlong dexterous fingers curled around the port rail. I pick him for a technologist.

I step forward and I see the tilt of his head as he hears me. I leave a body length between us and come to the rail, too. In the remnant glow of the engines, I can see that the wall outside is unnaturally smooth. So, not a crater after all. Someone punched this shaft in the surface. And at its base, there's a circle of pure black: a tunnel.

"Coryn Astridottir," says the Developer. "A task awaits us."

"Does it?" I say, with sarcasm, but something about him keeps my full disdain on a leash.

"Yes," he says. "Out there. Do you see?"

I don't want to see. I close my eyes and suck the air high into my sinuses. He smells faintly of lemon oil. They used to clean the labs with it, and that sharp scent peels a layer off my memory.

I sigh, wearily. "We've met before, haven't we?"

He turns to me, eyebrows popped in surprise above his pale yellow irises. I remember those eyes, but not from exactly when.

He hesitates, and glances back to the tunnel into the moon rock before he says, "You have denied memories. Why?"

I avoid that one. "How can I have met a Kraysis before? Your system is locked down."

He wrinkles his nose. "We do not call ourselves that."

He turns away from the portview and strides from the room. He's so fast that I think at first this is the end of the conversation, but One is expectantly waiting by the door, so I follow. Out into the hall, and around corners, and down a ladder into the cargo hold.

I hesitate when I see the ramp is down; there should be a sucking rush of the air escaping the ship down that ramp. There should be sirens, and popping ears, and closing bulkhead doors. At the very least, there should be a dream to wake up from.

But One stands to the side, a rigid sentry, and I know I'm expected to go outside in just my shipsuit.

Half-way down, I can smell the powder dust moon surface, dry silica high in my sinuses. The Developer is waiting at the ramp tip, his body a slender column throwing a compass-point shadow in the ship's lights. Above him is a faint shimmer, lofting in the air across the shaft. I'm guessing it's a membrane that's holding an atmosphere around the ship and that tunnel. Unless Earth-central has developed that in the last circle, I have a feeling no one outside the Kraysis system has seen this before.

As I step further, I can see the membrane's shimmer extends over the whole ship. The translucence of it between us and all that yawning space is unpleasant, as is the change from the ship's grav-deck to the moon's lower g. By the time I reach the Developer, my stomach is floating like a bubble, my balance a spinning compass.

The Developer seems impervious. He touches his ear and says to someone back on the ship, "Go and watch the agitator. I am taking the doctor to the vault."

And then he steps off the end of the ramp, his feet lifting puffs of moon dust that swirl like smoke.

〈〈〉〉

I fight the vertigo of altered-g down the tunnel, stumbling and tripping on nothing. My stomach turns over, mixing powdery moondust with the flood of saliva in my mouth. As that feeling finally ebbs, the Developer holds up a light, and around his long shadow, I can finally see the floor. The dust here is pushed up in ripples, like a pond frozen moments after a handful of cast-in stones. A delicate lacework pattern. Odd, very odd. Odder still to disturb it all with our feet.

The air is colder than on the ship, and dry, so dry, with that mineral-heavy dust. The irritation of the dryness occupies me at first, and we've gone a long way before I realize how my limbs don't have the usual bounce of moonwalking; there's more gravity here than I expected. A dense core on this moon, perhaps; or maybe that's just the hangover from the time spent with half of my brain offline.

The tunnel ends in a sheer wall from floor to roof with a glassy surface that glints in the light. I can make out patterns carved into the edifice: flowing symbols inscribed in quarter circles. I feel a shiver that reaches down to the pads of my toes. I mean, come on, a closed wall etched in alien script? At the end of a precision-cut tunnel? The deep fiber of me knows to be wary about a vault on the edge of the 'verse.

The Developer presses his palm to it, bowing his head. "This," he says, "is our task."

"Sorry. I forgot my pickaxe."

He lowers the light, and the symbols fade into shadow. "This barrier is refractory to all methods of excavation. It is formed of materials we have no experience with. We are left with opening the mechanism itself."

"What's in there? Some wealthy alien's sarcophagus?"

"The contents are not your concern. Our task is to open it."

"And what exactly do you want me to do about that?"

He makes a swift gesture, and suddenly the pressure on my chin releases, and the weight lifts from my head. A nucleus inside my brain begins fizzing, and then there's a thought ricochet as that other part of my mind comes online. I sway on my feet.

It takes a full minute before I feel as though there's one brain inside my head again, and not two. And with that whole comes that need of mine, uncurling unpleasantly in my body. The same one Riley has been satisfying since the *Freya*. Making up for the time it was offline. It's the one thing I didn't miss.

"Put your hands on the wall, doctor, and you will perceive the task."

I don't want to do what the Developer asks, but I want distraction. So I touch the stone.

At first, there's nothing. Not like if I was to put my hand to a ship's hull, and feel where the network of communication lines are. They peel out away from my hand like a hologram of the entire ship. Even when it takes time to tune in to the signals, they are always there. But a ship is light materials – metal and aerated ceramic. This wall is dense and old. But deep within it, if I strain my senses, there's a shape to find. A curving hairline arc through its immense thickness.

I hold my attention there, wondering how it is I can perceive a boundary in solid rock. And then, in my mind, that boundary *moves*, with a signal that ripples like an oil-stain shimmer on a vast lake. It curls on itself and, for just a moment, it feels like it could wriggle into my skin. I jerk my hand away. There's a lingering scent in my nose now, the smell of fusion engines burning rich.

"Ah, yes, you perceive it," the Developer says, sounding vindicated. "We have sufficient information to know the seal is biomechanical in nature. We believe you can open it."

I take a step backward, then another. "You Kraysis are the technologists. You don't need me for this."

He compresses his mouth, maybe because I used the name he doesn't like again, maybe something else. "On the balance of odds, we believe this is more expedient."

I read in his expression that they have tried other things and failed. And in studying his face so closely, other memories stir about him. They are very old, these memories. From the time just after I became what I am. He was an observer of some kind, I think. One of the many faces that looked on me from various vantages. He looked different, then. He passed easily for someone from the central systems. I wonder then how long the Kraysis have been infiltrating the rest of the 'verse, or if it was only him. Then my mind comes back to this vault, and how much longer than any of us existed it might have sat here. What kinds of reasons whoever built it might have had. And how it is that the Kraysis were the ones to find it.

"That waygate out there," I say slowly. "It's not running on the Earth-central system. It's yours."

"Ours," he says.

"I won't do it."

He changes the light into his other hand, looking down, then up, and back at me. Then he turns and retraces his steps through the moon dust. I stumble along, until we come to the mouth of the tunnel inside the shaft again, where the ship lights illuminate Riley, standing at the base of the ramp with One. The Developer stops. Before I know what's happened, the neural disruptor clamps back on my head. I feel the puff of moon dust as my knees hit the ground.

Through the fog of my grafted brain shutting down again, the Developer says, "You are free to refuse, of course. But if that is your choice, we will leave you here, and journey back through the waygate to find another such as you. By the time we return, you will be one with the dust in which you stand. A memory in any system you choose to name. You have the clock's rest to decide."

4

Riley and I are back in the bunk, but neither of us can rest. There's nothing I want more than to leave this moon behind. I resent the Kraysis to fiery solar hell for all of this.

I sit on the bunk, still feeling the weight of my body in the ship's grav-deck after the time on the moon outside. It's a reverse kind of sickness, squashing any food hunger against my spine. Riley is pacing, anger making his limbs jerk. I've never seen him like this. "Dusteaters," he says. "They'll do it. You know what they did when the Kraysis system broke away."

He means that glossed-over sentence in the histories.

"They gave non-friendlies an ultimatum to leave the system through the waygate," Riley says, in full rant. "But there were delays as all those ships tried to go through, and the waygate had to re-power and cycle between each one. When that deadline came, dozens of ships were still waiting to jump. They closed it anyway, and none of those ships were heard from again. We shouldn't be helping the Kraysis."

Quietly, I think that Earth-central left those ships in Kraysis space, too, probably without trying much on their behalf. The heavy end of authority is seldom able to negotiate with deft.

My reasons for not helping the Kraysis are far more personal: I am long past taking orders. But I also know that my choices are presently crushed in the Developer's fist, and the only way out might be through what he wants.

I try to refocus. "This end of the waygate traveled through interstellar space for decades to get here. It's the edge of the 'verse. Whoever made that vault, it wasn't us."

"So?"

"So what does it matter if it's Kraysis here first, or Earth-central?"

Riley shakes his head. "Kraysis have been dark for hundreds of circles. They've got tech we can't imagine and who knows what else. We shouldn't want them to get more of it."

I take a breath. "What do you know? And how?"

He clamps his next words before they can escape and says instead, "My point is, maybe this is something they created. Or that the covert sides of Earth-central could have brought out here. That's probably why the Kraysis want into it. Technology theft – that would be their style."

My eyes slide sideways. I've seen enough in my time in the central systems to entertain his theory. But the word theft jars, and I don't like the belligerence in him now, the hidden agenda. "Are you more worried about what's in there, or that the Kraysis see it before Earth-central?"

He's quiet then, exasperated with my lack of alignment to his own loyalties.

I however have dismissed the idea of making a stand against the Kraysis at this point, with its risk of them leaving us here. We'll last moments or hours, depending on whether that atmospheric membrane remains in tact. It's not the first time I've considered taking the low-odds option, but this is death with more certainty than any mortal agrees to.

I'm wondering if Riley is thinking the same when he says, "This ship has escape pods."

My head snaps up with a furious look. I point at the ceiling. The Kraysis are likely listening to all of this. We have to assume they are, so I can't believe Riley would be so careless to signal we might try for escape. He gives me a dirty look back, surprising me with his venom. There's something else in this interface between him and the Kraysis, something black with long roots. Something he hasn't said.

"Why do they want you?" Riley says after a long stretch of silence. "And not someone else?"

I stare out of the window port. "I met the Developer once, way back, though I don't exactly remember the details. And those incidents on the *Freya* and with the *Dellinger* were probably reported. I happened to be conveniently close to the near end of their waygate – wrong place, wrong time. Or the planetary powers don't want us to reach Earth, take your pick."

Riley shakes his head. I can tell that comment smarts him. He doesn't like defeatist views of this journey.

"They don't have augmentations, did you notice that?" he says. "No implants. They're still using bone conduction personal comms. If you don't do it, they can't themselves."

"Which still makes us dead, and them finding someone else, thank you."

My snap shuts the conversation down, and leaves a bad vibration between us, almost as ugly as the feeling of touching that wall, as the whiplash of having my brain augmentation turn on and off. The feeling simmers in rivulets of rage and remonstration. Normally, we would work this out between the covers, but with this thing on my head, I've no interest in him that way right now.

Fools fight when their enemy is right outside the door, so I wish I could talk into his head. Then I'd say, *if I do this, I can find out what I can. Look for an opportunity to escape, or send a message. Report this moon to the central systems.*

Instead, I write it, on one of Riley's offline screens, a word at a time that I delete as soon as I form it.

Riley writes back, *I could take them out*, which is about as much dusty shit as anyone can muster when talking about one man, even if he is ex-Special Ops, against at least three Kraysis, on their ship, and on the other side of their waygate, when said man has already admitted what tough bandits these Kraysis are. Riley might just be feeling suicidal, and the thought is an unexpected jolt, electric blue and painful.

So I write *NO* and to end this, I crack the screen through its middle. Then I lie on the bunk and close my eyes, resenting every moment that has led to this one.

After a long pause, in momentary truce, Riley says, "Could you sense what was inside that wall?"

I shake my head, curling round on myself. "I don't want to feel what's inside."

5

After the clock rest is over, One takes me back down the tunnel with a food bar in my hand. This time, I have the chance to observe more. The dust is dark gray and sparkling with minerals, the ripple-like patterns only visible in the shadows thrown from a glancing light. The Developer is waiting at the wall with a portable chair, a light stand, and a screen, ready to observe.

One removes the disruptor, and to hide the nausea of my brain coming fully back online, I point at the light and say, "You got one of those for me?"

The Developer rises smoothly, takes the light from its stand, and brings it to me. "Any tools you require, we will provide."

"Fast shuttle back to Jupiter Gate?"

"Humor is not presently a good use of your time."

"Then what about you bringing me Riley?"

"What do you want with the agitator?" he says.

I shrug. "To know where he is, for a start."

The Developer ponders a long moment before he signals One to return to the ship. I'm relieved; I want Riley here where I can keep an eye on him, where he could do something useful, rather than festering subversive plans in the bunk. He arrives a few minutes later, wary surprise written in his modded eyes.

The Developer considers him. "What will you have your companion do?"

"Look around," I say, pointing to the carvings on the wall surface. "See if he can find any more marks like these ones."

"I assure you, we have taken a detailed survey," the Developer says.

"Doesn't hurt to repeat."

The Developer argues no further, and Riley goes off with a

screen in hand. I turn back to the wall, and press a palm into the surface, searching for that shape I sensed yesterday, even though I'm not sure I want that shimmering vast-lake feeling again.

It's there, a semi-circle arching high above my head. I avoid lingering in one place this time, and as I move along the wall, I find where the curve of it comes down to touch the sides of the tunnel. The wall covering this internal shape looks no different to the rest, and I can detect no seam under my fingers, but that faint signal is there underneath: the edge of the vault opening.

But the amplitude is so small. I have to strain my senses just to perceive that shimmering signal at the surface. It's not just small: it's noisy, confused. I don't find that feeling of a vast lake again; just this muddled vibration. I spend an hour this way, tiring myself out, moving back and forth, hoping to find a place where the signal is easier to read. Maybe the vault has some kind of noise generator to prevent this kind of entry.

The Developer sits silent for all this time. He seems eager to ask what I've found, but is well trained in allowing another person to work.

Finally, I put both my hands over the surface, and lean my forehead between them, throwing out my broadcast as far as I can.

The next thing, I'm sitting on my ass, rubbing my forehead.

"What was that?" The Developer has shot to his feet, but doesn't come to my aid.

"Finally got a stronger signal," I say, feeling the echo of the wave that just hit me between my sensory eyes. It lingers with that smell of fusion engines again, and this time, something else: a fading sound of running feet. "The bioresonance signal had too low an amplitude to make any sense of it."

"Until you did what?"

"Used maximum projection of my broadcast."

The Developer taps a rapid finger against his cheek. "So the signal increased when your projection energy increased … it is possible, then, the bioresonance is passive, and requires energy input to excite its amplitude and create the interface."

I nod slowly. "That would make sense for a vault – require someone to put energy in. Then it always fails closed. But if that's true, I'm not going to be able to do much with this. I can't sustain that kind of projection for more than a moment."

But the Developer is excitedly tapping on his screen, and a minute later, Two and Three come jogging down the tunnel. He hands them the neural disruptor. "Find another like this and take it the development studio, then bring this one back."

After they have gone, he says, "I will reverse the polarity of the disruptor so that it can enhance your signal projection. We will test it after the next clock's rest. Until then, describe to me in detail everything else you observed in the wall."

As I do so, I'm thinking in parallel about the speed of the Developer's logic, the capabilities he must have on the ship, all while realizing they are never going to let me back on board without the disruptor in place.

❮❯

There's hot food waiting for us in the bunk when the Developer sends us back to the ship. One keeps more than the usual distance from us, and hovers in the hall, as if waiting on some purpose. I step out, expecting her to speak, but she steps away quickly, as if caught in some misdemeanor.

Riley is picking over the food, which smells more rich and filling than standard spaceliner fare. There's some kind of root vegetable mashed with warm spices, and a soup that tastes as if it didn't come from powder. A bowl of leaves is dark green with nutrients, fresh from a garden that must be somewhere on board. But there's less taste than I expected. I chew slowly, poring over whether it's the food itself, or the dry moon dust in my nose, or because of the disruptor. Everything about my senses seems blunted with it on. Riley doesn't touch the food at all.

"What did you find?" I finally ask.

"They look at you funny."

"Who?"

He nods toward the open door, not bothering to lower his voice much. His lengthening hair nods against his forehead. "Them. The Three. They look at you funny."

"Funny how?" I say, thinking about One hovering in the hall.

"Like they've never seen anything like us before."

"Maybe they haven't."

He makes a face.

I sigh. "Anything else?"

He says, "Those patterns in the floor dust go all the way down the side passages off the main tunnel, until those passages end in the wall, too."

"What side passages?"

"The ones that come off the main tunnel," he repeats slowly, as if I'm neutron-dense. "The ones I guess you haven't seen."

I sit back, considering. The Kraysis really don't rate Riley as a threat if they're prepared to let him wander about tunnels unsupervised. Then again, how much trouble could he get in to?

"What made the patterns?" Riley asks. "They look like ripples. Or waves."

"An interference pattern, yes. I was thinking the same thing, but I don't know. This place could have been here millions of years in the same state it is now."

Riley grunts. But those patterns are before my eyes again now, a dark lacework puzzle.

"I should look at those other patterns," I say. "Maybe they mean something. It might give us a clue about the vault."

Riley takes a breath, and I realize I've made some kind of misstep without really registering what it is. Then he pushes off the bunk, the muscles of his back bunching under his shirt. I've never seen those muscles do that before without wanting them above me. He turns in the door.

"Sometimes, Coryn, you sound like you want to open this thing," he says, and that's the end of the conversation.

6

After the next clock's rest, when I reach the end of the tunnel, the Developer is waiting with another neural disruptor. Riley was right – as I came down the tunnel today, I noted the side passages, extending from shallow recesses in the tunnel. I can't think why I didn't perceive them before. I can certainly see the evidence I passed here in my earlier tracks that have smudged away the patterns in the moon dust. That same moon dust has turned the path through the cargo hold gray, which I saw Three trying and failing to clean. I have an uncomfortable thought that parts of this moon will be with us forever.

Riley trails behind me, still aggrieved, and keeps his distance when the Developer holds out the new disruptor.

"As promised," he says. "With reversed polarity to augment your broadcast signal."

"What made all these patterns in the dust?" I ask, not taking the disruptor.

He gives a slight shrug. "We theorize they are settling patterns following an asteroid impact within the crater and subsequent shock waves reverberating off the tunnel wall structure. The material in here appears to have unique reflective properties. Or, a similar phenomena, but resulting from the thrust engines of a craft departing the shaft."

I think about that smell of fusion engines I had last clock, probably part of my desire to leave this place. I take the head-gear.

While I'm not in a mood to replace one set of chains for another, I have to admit that his application is sound. The new head-gear removes the strain. What yesterday felt might burst a blood vessel, today is effortless. Even the g-change nausea seems more settled. It takes less than an hour for me to work along the vault door seam and amplify the latent vibrational pattern in its interface. With the augmentation, what I find is clear: there's not one signal, but many.

I step back from the wall, my fists in my hips. "Why did you choose me for this?"

"You are rumored to be the best."

I snap a look at him. "Then you should also have heard that flattery doesn't work on me."

The Developer shifts on his feet, seeming abashed. It's the first time I've seen him uncomfortable. "It is not normally in our nature to offer such comments," he says finally.

"So why do it?"

"Some other developers suggested that compliments may assist in persuading your cooperation," he says. "I shall be sure to note they were mistaken."

I snort. At least we're clear on one thing. And the Developer's mouth has an odd curve at the corners now. Not a smile, but something close to amusement at least. I suspect this is rare in a tense type like him. I imagine him as one in a group of like-positioned Kraysis, where he perhaps isn't one of the crowd. It thaws me toward him, just a little.

"This interface," I say. "The vibrational pattern appears multi-modal, many signals overlaid on each other. I can bring most of them out by changing the frequency I'm broadcasting on, but not all at once. And there's still noise in there."

"A lock with many keys," the Developer says. "Yes, such complexity would be expected."

He taps his finger against his cheek again, his eyes shifting in a sideways staccato, as if he's speed-reading down a text. Then his pupils fix on mine. "Perhaps, we can make further adjustments to the neural device. In addition to the power gain, we could add a frequency split. We will need to adjust it as you discover the frequencies, but eventually, we will have all the keys."

"Won't that drop the power to each frequency?" I say.

He nods. "We would need to increase the gain further, to compensate. This I can do."

My body tingles unpleasantly. One of the effects of the higher gain model I'm currently wearing is an increase in the pressure from that demanding need my brain graft creates. It's already becoming a burdensome distraction, so I want to wrap this up and either find a warm body to satisfy it, or put that other brain prison back on, to chain it down again.

I realize the Developer is staring at me. "There is something you are not saying."

No shit. But I'm not about to tell him about that particular issue. "There's something you're missing," I say instead.

He waits, expectant.

"Even if we manage to excite all these latent frequencies in the vault lock, how do you know that it will open? If you don't know who built this place, how do you know the mechanism works? Or that there's even a mechanism? This could be just some residual signal. Someone's weird data library from another time."

That, at least, would explain the fusion engine scent which still enters my senses when touching the wall, and that occasional glitch I get of running feet. Residual data is a much nicer idea than hallucination.

"We are confident that when all the frequencies are correctly excited, the vault will open."

"Based on what?"

"We don't think that's relevant to your task."

"It's relevant if you want me to keep trying."

He hesitates then, sitting back down on his little portable seat. Staring at him, I wonder about the other developers he mentioned, the other Kraysis. How many layers of command might be above him?

All I really knew about Kraysis came from rumors percolating through the 'verse on overheard lips: that they were advanced technologically, but backward culturally. Militaristic, violent, isolationist. But did that really say anything about them? Who knew what was really happening back in their closed system, in those moons and planets? The Developer could be the lowest rung in their culture, sent on a low-odds mission only deemed of minor importance. Or he could be their demigod.

Either way, right now I have a feeling he's searching through the consequences of answering my question, and weighing them against the odds they will help us succeed.

"Based on the preliminary investigations of other developers," he says slowly, "and comparing the architecture of the latent vibrations in the vault door to signatures we observed in other bioresonance projects."

"What other bioresonance projects?"

He shifts on his feet again. His nose wrinkles, just slightly, a tiny sign of disgust. "In the central systems."

"You mean, us," I say, suspecting he's referring to the line of bioresonance engineered experiments created by a particular arm of the central systems' think-tanks. The same ones that produced the *Dellinger*, that produced me, and a dozen other questionable successes. From the same time period I met this Developer. So no prizes for who recognized the similarity between the vault's material system and what my head could do.

"I guess that piece of espionage came in handy," I say.

"We do not use that word," he says. "It is not *espionage* to protect a society against the evils another might wreck on it—"

He cuts himself off, a look of surprise on his face, as if he's been too well trained to forget that he shouldn't say such things to the infidels.

"Don't stop on my account," I say, wondering if he might be about to reveal something to fill in the gaps I have about the Kraysis, the uncomfortable holes that always exist in a story that's only ever been told from one side. Riley would be looking for chances in those gaps, something he could exploit to send a communication, and hope for rescue. And I am too. But I'm also curious.

The Developer however turns and picks up the chair, and his light stand, and sweeps back down the tunnel. I can't tell whether he's in a hurry to escape my presence, or to undertake some self-flagellation. Either way, I seem off the hook for now.

❰❮❯❱

Riley is waiting at the end of the tunnel when I finally trek back to the mouth. From his rigid posture, I know that something is going on, and immediately I see that the ramp to the Kraysis ship is closed.

"What are they doing?" I ask, with a shot of dread.

Riley shakes his head, as though tension has blocked all his words. He's had the same that nightmare I've had, of standing in this spot watching their engines burning away against that punched-out hole of black sky above. But the engines now are dark. There's not even any metallic smell of a craft warming up. There's only soft light from a few port windows, and a gentle hum of power running through wires that probably only I can hear.

It's the first time I've really looked at the ship since we first boarded. It has the conglomerate look of many spacefaring craft that can land on moons, and anywhere the atmosphere is pretty thin, but there's something different about it, too. That wouldn't be noticed at a glance. It's as though the Kraysis have imitated a central systems ship they saw without being able to erase their own unique styling. But the copying means plenty is familiar.

At heart, most spacefaring ships are similarly configured. Fusion drive at the core with the engines behind that. All the life-support systems are on top for a manned boat, or replaced with automation systems on an unmanned one. Quarters and laboratories and crew spaces will fit out the scaffold space, wrapping about three-quarters around. The remaining quarter on the side of the drive is where the escape pods sit – the theory being that in the event of using them, you can shield the boats with the bulk of the fusion drive. On the starboard here I see the standard bay doors for escape pods. The bridge, on the other hand, is always somewhere up front – central, or to one side, or high, depending on the shape of the ship's scaffold.

This ship has a high one. Above the forward viewing port is a forward-thrust knob like a thick neck and just behind it, a smooth band in the structure bristles with spikes. That's probably the communications array, which is where Riley's attention is fixed.

"Do you—" I begin, then stop. *Do you have any plans?*

As I speak into his mind, something I haven't been able to do since they first slapped that disruptor on my head, something instantly relaxes between us.

Maybe, he says back, but he sounds less confident than when he was proposing drastic action a few clocks ago.

I run my eye over the rest of the craft. It occupies about a third of the space in the bottom of this shaft, so it must have full vertical capabilities in low gravity. I can see what look like thermal sink bulkheads on the port side – probably for a greenhouse. And on the very top level, I see a bank of lit port windows. Every few seconds, I see a shadow pass over one of them. I imagine the Developer up there, pacing in his workspace. I wonder what it looks like.

If they were going to leave, I think they would have by now, I say, hoping it's true.

Riley is silent for a long while before he says, *You don't know Kraysis.*

But they don't leave. Eventually, just as I'm about to suggest to Riley that we go back into one of the deep passages, a band of alert lights flicker on, and the ramp slowly descends. This time, it's Two who emerges with the neural disruptor. He must have been the one to draw lots today, because he disappears as quickly as he can after ensuring we go back to the bunk.

Food is waiting again, only this time the green soup is tepid, and the flatbread alongside it raw in the middle.

"Must have really ticked him off," I say, rolling a ball of dough around in my fingers. The higher-g is again displacing my hunger. "This is what the mess cooks used to do when someone hadn't shown the proper respect."

Riley warms slightly. "Ours, too," he says. "There was this one time …"

And then it's like he suddenly remembers we're on an enemy spacecraft at the far end of the 'verse, being pressganged to open an alien vault, and without any prospect of rescue, and that there's no nostalgic story from his past light enough to overcome the weight of that.

We pick at the meal in silence and Riley's the one pretending to sleep when a shadow appears in the doorway: the Developer himself. His eyes fall quickly on Riley, before he says, "Join me in the workspace."

‹‹ › ›

The Developer's workspace is the top level of the ship with the ports I saw from outside. There's no pretense in here that this is an Earth-central systems ship. The architecture is angular, with triangle ports that ring the roof, providing a sense of endless night to work in. The tables hang from the ceiling on stiff rods, the floor uncluttered. One wall is filled with shelves of clear tubs: some full of shining silver loops, others with dark black powders that shimmer with colored iridescence, others still with clay-like lumps. The other end wall is arrayed with screens, and the two walls in between with mysterious doors and buttons. Screens aside, I have no idea what any of it is.

The Developer folds two chairs up from the floor, and invites me to sit. Under all the port windows, it feels like a tent out in the desert, which I experienced a long time ago, in a place where there was more sand than water, and the sky was a black canvas of untroubled stars.

"I apologize about the quality of your meal," he begins. "There was some malfunction with the galley. And we have not spared technician time to fix it."

I raise my eyebrows. "And here I was thinking it was punishment for some kind of insolence."

The Developer frowns. "Withholding food is never a productive technique for enticing a captive to cooperate," he says. "If you have gone to the trouble to preserve someone's life, then you preserve it."

"Really," I say, unconvinced. "You know, Riley is pretty good with technical faultfinding."

The Developer shakes his head softly, and I shrug. It was worth a try.

But then the Developer shifts his feet again, clearly trying to broach a subject. I take the time to study him. Riley is right. There's no evidence of augmentation – no ridges or scars in the usual places at temples and wrists. Just the bone conduction comms over his ears, the type that only touch skin.

"I am uncomfortable about something in our earlier

conversation," he says at length. "Many among us believe it protects us to remain separated from the Earth-central systems, but some of us believe it will ultimately lead to greater aggression from them. Such as when they sent forces against us."

I try not to betray surprise. Earth-central sent forces? Was that what Riley knew about?

"I think Earth-central would be the ones thinking the Kraysis are aggressive," I say. "You've taken us as captives. That's an act of war."

"At the time of our break with Earth-central, there was not another option. Our technologies were being stolen."

"Stolen?"

"That is what you call it, is it not, when someone else takes something you have without your permission?"

"I'd say it amounts to the same thing as taking people hostage. But if you were part of the Earth-central systems back then, all technology was shared by mandate. To benefit everyone, and everyone knows that."

The Developer's nose wrinkles again. "In word of law, perhaps. And grav-deck technology should certainly have been shared—"

"Grav-deck technology?"

He pauses, as if offended. "You did not know the grav-deck was created in our workspaces?"

This was news to me, and he might be lying. In the early decades of the off-Earth systems, lifespans of the Intrepid – the willing migrants – were only just long enough to raise the next generation of poorly adapted to low-g humans. It must have been miserable, living that way. But then had come the grav-deck, a brilliant technology that didn't rely on mass to create gravity. Didn't rely on simulating it with rotating mouse-wheel ship designs. Instead, it excited the gravity field itself, making everything within its effect zone experience a gravitational pull. But that technology came from the ancient labs on Earth. I suppose the Kraysis system was already colonized with Intrepid before the grav-deck, so what he's saying isn't impossible, but it's hard to rewrite the history you learned first.

"It's not the story that Earth-central tells," I say, which is truth at least.

"When our children were being denied basic supplies, and we denied basic representation in central decision-making, the grav-deck was our break point. Our technologies were going out to central, but nothing was coming back. We created the things that built the 'verse, and central just pushed us down harder. You don't continue to supply an oppressor like that. You say, *no*. You leave their oppression."

I rub at my temples, feeling the discomfort of knowing we're about to enter into the political history of an entire people and their arguments with Earth-central. That topic could be broached by a native of any of the first or second orders of off-Earth systems, and leave a floor decorated with blood and teeth. Let alone a Kraysis, the only second-generation system to actually shut Earth-central out. Their arguments must run to legion.

"Are you telling me this because of the vault?" I say.

He takes a long breath, and looks up into those black ports over us, as if he realizes he has strayed from his purpose and is only returning to it with great reluctance.

"When we locked down the Earth-central waygate," he says. "We locked ourselves into our system. We did that to protect ourselves from our oppressors. We kept our value behind that wall. And we believe that is also true of this vault."

"So now you want to raid someone else's cache?"

"This place is long abandoned," he says quickly. "Our readings on the isotopes indicate it was sealed while humans were still learning to walk upright. We have long passed a horizon where any of us consider this theft. It is more akin to archaeology, such as in the ancient tombs of old Egypt."

"No tomb ever had a bioresonance lock," I say. "How do you know what's in there isn't dangerous? We put prisoners behind walls."

"*We* don't, actually. You will note that we do not lock your bunk. And even Earth-central prisons are not vaults. They have people who circulate through. They have visitors."

Some prisons, I think. Not all.

"Still," I say.

"If this really were something dangerous," he says, "why would the builders create a way to open it?"

I think about that for a few beats, then I say, "Why aren't there more of you here, to document the process?"

"My records are sufficient."

But the way he says it, the way he swallows, I wonder if he chose this situation for himself, or if he is as unwilling a participant as I am.

He says, "I am of the position that it is good to look behind walls, to see what goes on beyond. Such as in the central systems."

I tip my head to the side. "Is that why I've met you before?"

"Why do you think we speak standard dialects so well? And still build ships to resemble central system models? We have been among you for as long as we've had our waygate closed." He takes a breath, and I know he is not meant to talk of these things. "We believe in knowing our oppressors better than they know themselves."

"Except for the implants, the man-machine interfaces."

The look of distaste comes on him again. "That, we will never do. Augmentations are the technology of Earth-central. When you invite something into your body, you have to accept the possibility it will control you."

I stare at him for a long string of heartbeats, feeling the truth in that statement. We've more in common than I could have expected.

"And this vault," I say, "you don't want to open it just to liberate the contents from biomechanical control? Some kind of cultural crusade?"

He sits back as though this is an entirely new idea, one he finds troubling. "Perhaps this talk is at an end."

I rise to go, sensing the conversation is at an end, but the opinion I had of the Kraysis before this meeting has shifted. As I stand, I feel a wobble in the gravity field, with the tiny burst of free-fall nausea. Even the Kraysis systems aren't perfect.

As I reach the door he says, "Not all of us think of Earth-central the same. But regardless of that, we are here to open this vault, and find what it might contain for the benefit of all."

But as I walk back to the bunk, I know that by *all* he means the Kraysis, and to solar hell with the rest of us.

❮❬❭❯

"Savage," is Riley's retort to the Developer's claims about the vault. "You put dangerous things in a prison, and they have doors."

"I made that point," I say. "But you're both missing the full scope. I can think of at least six reasons to build a vault like this one. Both of you seem to think the 'verse hangs on two ends of a long balance. You should have seen enough to know that's not true."

He's silent a beat, then he says, "You've never fought against them. They're hardened – none of the EM disruptors worked. None of the shields. If they ever chose to come back across their waygate—"

"What, they'd take over the 'verse?"

He turns away.

"When did you fight against them?" I ask. "If they've been closed down for hundreds of circles. You telling me those stories about them raiding systems is true?"

I have a hard time seeing the Developer as a 'verse conqueror. Then again, many people have slipped around my radar for who they were. The last one ended up taking the *Dellinger* in his spare cyborg drive to that reconditioner we left in the last system, and the two of them are probably heading back to Earth-central now. The one before was a militant who orchestrated a coup on the infected *Freya*, nearly getting thousands of people killed. I'm not exactly to be trusted when it comes to people. Machines are a much easier read.

"Those stories are true." He rubs a hand across his face, and I see in the strain of his expression that he's fighting conditioning not to disclose operational secrets. "But we've been back to their space, too."

"When?"

"Earth-central pushed a new waygate across space to their system. They told us it had been carefully plotted so its approach would be hidden behind light-scattering cloud. I was in the forward battalion that would secure a path down to the homeworld. We were told there were old colonial controls that would be activated to subdue the population. We were told our approach would be unnoticed. That the taking of the planet would be done within a few clocks. Instead, we came through into an ambush. They knew we were there, and like I said, our weapons weren't much good against them. But theirs ... our instruments didn't know which way to spin. They would tell us there was nothing out there, and then a singularity would suddenly appear on the grav-map, alarms going crazy. Their ships could scatter starlight. They had complex field disruption that Earth-central was still only experimenting with. After two clocks hunkered down on a moon, us techs worked out how to shield our instruments from their disruptors, but they'd already moved on to other tactics."

"Like what?"

"Laying false beacons. They'd mimic our ship distress call, right down to the encrypted authority, and when our recovery would come to help, they'd be disappeared out of the sky. Not blown up, just ... vanished. We started leaving ships behind because no one trusted the beacons anymore."

He can't go on then, and I understand something of why. Those Special Ops guys have a code. They don't leave people behind, just like Riley wouldn't leave me behind on the *Freya*.

"I'm sorry," I say, but I don't know how to comfort him, because like I said, machines are my read, and there's no comfort here with the Kraysis. Riley's better off alone.

I get up, deciding I'll make use of the open door and walk around this ship, even if the only senses I have are the ones I came into the 'verse with.

As I reach the door, Riley says, "You said six reasons. What are the other four?"

I sigh. "A prison or a safe aren't airtight. This place is. So, what's behind there could be in a different state – under different pressure or atmosphere or temperature, right? Therefore, the reasons are one, to keep something alive. Two, to keep something inert. Three, to protect something dormant, like a seed."

"And last?"

I shrug. "Maintain a state until someone can work out what to do with it. Like cryo, or the ancient waste stores on Earth-central."

"That's the same as dormant," Riley says.

"No, it's not. Cryo, someone's got to wake you up. Dormant things know how to wake up on their own."

Then I walk away down the hall, hearing the breath going in and out of my body, louder than my footfalls.

7

It takes three clocks to tune in and record all the frequencies I can find in the material. Each time, the Developer returns wordlessly to the ship to adjust his neural device to amplify my resonance capability on those frequencies. But even when he's locked in all the frequencies, there's still noise in the signals, a constant background buzzing that shows up whenever I push my senses into the vault wall.

In between, Riley and I barely speak in the bunk, and courtesy of the galley problem, there's not even any hot food to stay for. With the dim lights, it's too cozy for the mood between us. So I've taken to going out into the ship every rest, scuffing my boots over the hallways of Kraysis-made material. Steps barely make sound on their surfaces, and they have a *give* underfoot. It reminds me of walking on a forest floor, which I last did too long ago, though it smells of clinical lemons here and not of leaves and earth.

Many parts of the Kraysis ship have a smell of fruit. Something like apples wafts from the locked doors in the cargo hold. I smell oranges on my hands after running my fingers along the door to the ship's plant room. It's right by the greenhouse, and we're locked out of both. Fair enough – it contains most of the ship's critical infrastructure, except for the engines, batteries and the grav-deck.

My walk always ends back around the perimeter hall into the mirror side of the ship, where I run into a closed bulkhead door. The lights are bright here, the piercing blue of a new-born star. They must be running on a different power system to the dull midlife yellow of the ones on the other side of the ship. From those two clues, I assume behind the bulkhead door are the escape pods. There's two other closed doors like this – one is on the accessway up to the Developer's workspace; the other leads up into the bridge.

The lights up there are barely glowing. I haven't seen circadian cycle protection like that since the last Earth-central military ship I was on. But the important point is the door. If I had the disruptor off, I could gain access, and maybe enough access to barricade myself inside the bridge and fly the ship right off this moon. And if Riley could access the system, he probably could, too.

The Kraysis know this.

They've ensured we can't do anything except what they've asked.

《〈〉》

The breakthrough comes in the next clock. I'm off task, thinking about anything rather than that uncomfortable need that keeps unfurling in my body. This time, my thoughts stray to the Kraysis ship, and the grav-deck wobble I felt last clock in the Developer's workspace, and that's when I have the idea.

It starts from remembering the indignation of the Developer when he talked about how the grav-deck was stolen from the Kraysis. That emotion had reminded me of another cloudy person from the distant past: a physicist teacher we had in the academy. Grav-deck technology was something he mentioned often, which itself wasn't unusual – all the physicists were mad for the grav-deck. What was unusual was him going off one day on a recruit, a slimy man I didn't much like called Weaver, over how Weaver thought about the 'verse all wrong. That is was a field universe, not a particle universe. Most of what he'd been screaming I couldn't remember, but I remember the word 'vector' being deployed among the swearing.

Vectors matter a lot in space, including for the grav-deck – it's not just about how much g you have, but in which direction, just as it matters for boosting engines and a dozen other things. You need the right amount, pointing the right way. Pretty basic.

But now, thinking about directionality and these signals latent in the vault, I feel a qualm.

Until now, I've been sensing them the way I do the signals in a ship's comms lines, using the interface in the stone as my reference direction. But this isn't a comms line. Hell, it isn't even an interface that I had any evidence of.

I step back from the wall with the whole way I've been conceiving of this problem spinning on its axis.

"What?" asks the Developer.

I don't answer him. Instead, I pull the neural enhancer off my head. When I put my hands back to the wall, I try to empty out the very idea of the vault, the idea of the door. I probe at the edges of that imagined interface. It's hard without the enhancer to boost my broadcast, but it also means those boosted signals aren't dominating either. Steadily, I realize that there are other latent vibrations in there, lying across the ones I'd been thinking of as the arch of the 'door'. Across them, and through them in all directions.

This was what I had thought was noise. It wasn't. It was a three-dimensional pattern.

I stand back from the wall.

"You have made a breakthrough," the Developer says, and the excitement in his voice tells me a realization is showing on my face.

"I'm not sure," I hedge. "I think there are more frequencies, different to the ones I already found."

The Developer stills, then he says, "Are you sure?"

There's opportunity here to stall, but I find myself telling him. "What I thought was noise – I think those are latent vibrations in other signal planes."

The Developer is on his feet now. "It is as we hoped," he says softly. "It is a genuine field. A new kind of field material."

"A field material?"

"Yes, one that is capable of storing a signal in its field structure. Perhaps in multiple interrelated field structures."

I look back at the wall, which looks for all the moons in all the systems like glass-faced rock. "I don't follow."

"That's because you learned from Earth-central physicists, who still teach about particles. There are no particles. There are only excitations in fields. Local excitations, and wave excitations, and fields interacting with one another. Resonating, transferring energy. Like those used for the grav-deck, only for fields besides matter."

He stops himself and looks at me, hesitatingly, as if he has gone too far.

"If you say so," I say, and this time my lie slides smoothly between us. But I'm feeling the strangeness of coincidence – that I should have thought of that old physicist ranting about fields and vectors just before, and now have the Developer say very similar things. As if he's in my head.

But now I know why the Kraysis are interested in this vault. Materials are their thing – they've done that better than Earth-central technologists from the beginning, from the grav-deck to aerogels. Now they want what's in this vault – not for what it *is* but for what it's made of. My stomach rolls with foreboding, because anytime you stop looking at all a thing is … that's when mistakes happen. Misunderstandings. Miscalculations. And you can't always see those until it's too late.

I have an urge to escape as fast as a comet in a gas-giant gravity assist.

"I'm not sure there's really a seam in the wall at all," I say. "And there might be dozens of vector frequencies to find."

But the Developer isn't listening. He has his momentum now. He's caught in the gravity of his task's end and is speeding toward it.

❬❬❭❭

"I don't like it," I say to Riley later in the bunk, the neural disruptor rubbing against my neck. "This thing is weirder than anything I've ever seen. And that's saying something."

"I found something, too," he says. "I'm sure there were glyphs carved into the wall in one of the side passages, but they're gone now. And those patterns on the floor? They're changing."

"Changing how?"

"The pattern's shifting. And in some places, I could swear they reformed where I'd walked. There's no weather to explain that."

I frown at him. "Reformed?"

"I could swear. Only, and get this, if I take a picture of a location, those patterns I've recorded *don't* change."

My frown deepens. This sounds more like mirages than evidence. But still, the idea sticks in my thoughts like moon dust against my skin, chafing at an idea long forgotten. There's too much coincidence … bioresonance material in a vault door with patterns all over the floor.

"They could be Chladni," I say finally, pulling the word from a deep memory that must have snuck around the neural disruptor.

"What's that?"

"Patterns in materials when they're vibrating in different frequency modes. Dump a bunch of fine dust on a vibrating plate and you can see them."

What I don't say is that I know this only because Chladni are similar to Faraday waves in liquids, which is one of the microscale assembly techniques they used to make my autologous brain graft. Back then, before it had actually happened, I'd been an enthusiastic recruit, learning all I was allowed to know about what would be done to me.

Well, that was before.

"So the surface under that moon dust is vibrating? Doesn't feel like it."

"Doesn't feel like it when we're walking on it, you mean."

We absorb the implications of that.

"So you're saying," Riley says slowly, "that whatever's in that vault could be causing a vibration selectively, knowing when we're there and when we're not. And knowing when I've made a recording of it."

"If it is, what do we do about it?" I say finally.

Riley sighs. "They will just bring someone else. Kraysis don't waver. If these ones fail, more will come."

"Then we'd better hope that what we find in there is a dusty sarcophagus," I say. One without a curse.

8

Riley is right: the Developer is completely uninterested in the possibility of the patterns changing. Or, he pretends to be.

It takes three clocks for him to fashion the neural enhancer to add variable directionality to its signals. The thing gets bulkier each time, with little tumorous growths of accessory modules hanging off it. Seeing that on the outside gives me an uncomfortable feeling of what actually went on inside my head when they made me what I am. Neural resonance technology wasn't exactly mature back then, and they abandoned some of the things they gave us early recruits for a reason. But I've never stared those reasons down before, and I'm not about to start. I stare instead at the patterns in the tunnel dust, daring them to move. They never do, and I begin to believe Riley is mistaken.

With the ugly mug of the neural enhancer in place, on the fourth clock I'm finally before that vault door with the sense there is nothing left to discover in the latent frequencies. I glance at the Developer. His eyes have sunk and laced with red, resting on the purple cushions of his cheek skin. He has been up long into rest time making modifications and is not at his prime. I guess the circadian lights aren't enough for him, and that he never had my schooling. In the months after I was made, sleep cycles were emphasized for recovery and graft success, for alertness and attention. Going without wasn't seen as toughness; it was stupidity, risking the investment Earth-central had made in each of us. It's a habit I've kept. Maybe it's one of the habits the Kraysis rejected, too symbolic of Earth-central. And if that's true, I wonder at the decisions made by a legion of Kraysis without sleep.

"Go ahead," he says.

"You don't want to … prepare first?" I say.

"Why, do you sense what is inside?"

I don't sense anything except the perfect resonance of all the frequencies of the material under my hand. The signals no longer have noise. The pattern is elegant, interlaced and perfect in its clarity. It's mindbending and beautiful to hold it in my senses. It makes me feel a way I've only ever felt a handful of times … the first time I saw a rose bloom in a greenhouse, the first time I stood under a simulated redwood. The only time I smelled the inside of a real vanilla bean. I'm keeping the pattern at a low amplitude for now, but the shape of it is still almost therapeutic, a massaging vibration inside my head.

I suspend in that feeling, stretching this moment out and out. I blink, and remember another sensation like it, of hanging out of a bay-door in orbit over a blue and white world.

Then I realize I've gone somewhere else. This isn't my memory. There's a strange smell in the suit I'm wearing, something like cloves, which is what bathrooms always smelled like on the first starships I ever traveled on. I push my broadcast out, and feel the vibrations respond, others exciting and joining, a tangle of resonant modes that promises importance. A critical energy that wants to be reached. And just as I do, time pauses.

I look around. The tunnel floor is shaking, smooth moon dust vibrating into those lace patterns all over again. There's no longer a wall under my hand, but there are voices. They are speaking a language I can't understand, but fear and urgency are in their words and steps. They are cold. I feel a diamond grid of it needling my skin. I try to turn my head enough to see where they've come from, but their ship remains a dark shape out of view. The only shape I can make out is a sphere, then another. And another. They are carrying them, down into the vault. And then they are building this wall with a device I've never seen before, a shuttle that skims around the opening weaving a black crystal surface etched with symbols.

Something isn't right here. The thought flutters in my chest like the final throe of a spent power cell, and then I'm through the critical energy level, and all the vibrations in the wall material align.

There's a shift, which feels in my head the same way that

turning an old lock feels in the hand. The vibrations collapse, then the channel is suddenly gone. My head rings with the silence.

I step back from the wall, feeling depleted and emotional, in a way I'm careful never to be. Whatever went down here may have happened eons ago, but the residue of that time is somehow locked into this wall as if it were only a clock back.

The Developer looks at me, bruised eyes expectant under raised brows. To my left, at the mouth of one of the side passages, I see Riley standing sentry.

"It's done," I said. "I think."

The Developer looks at the wall, up that sheer obsidian black of it. He sees the same thing I do. Nothing has changed.

❰❮❯❱

We've been confined to the bunk for hours now. Hours since the Developer and his three minions scoured every accessible face of the wall for a sign of an opening that couldn't be found. The Developer had me check three times that the vibration signal had gone, and I lost my temper when he began to insinuate it was some kind of ruse on my part. It was only when Riley began to raise his theories about the patterns on the floor shifting again that the Developer sent us back to the ship, but not before putting the disruptor back on me. He may have been belligerent in his fatigue and his failure, but not stupid.

It's cold in here; no doubt our thermal comfort is now set by the Developer's mood.

Riley and I have been having a furious conversation on an offline screen for a whole hour, speculating about what will happen next, and Riley's attempts to access the ship's systems every clock since we've been here, when Riley tenses and smoothly slides the screen into the bunk cover. The Developer appears in the door and summons me with a stare.

We walk to the ship's ramp in silence where he stops, moodily facing the mouth of the tunnel below us. "I must offer you apologies," he says, but stiffly, as if this costs him dearly. "Perhaps the mechanism in the opening no longer functions, after all this time has passed."

"Perhaps there is no mechanism," I say, thinking on that ancient memory that unfolded itself in my head from the wall, though I won't tell the Developer about that. I don't want to give him reason to go poking around in my mind. He is clearly distracted by his failure, desperate to correct it.

"We will continue to examine every facet," he says, with more shake than assurance. "Until we are sure no change has been wrought."

"And what about us?"

"The time to complete our evaluation will also ensure we have identified the power supply problem to the galley. We like to return our ships in full working order."

The way he skips across my question gives me a qualm. I think about the situation from his perspective. We've been taken into the depths of what must be a secretive Kraysis mission. Through one of their waygates, not one controlled by Earth-central. We have seen the inside of their ship, done their bidding. The Developer has admitted things to me. If they let us go, we could report any of it to Earth-central.

I figure, at best, they plan to take us back to the Kraysis system for whatever useful purpose we might have. At worst, they will make good on their original threat to leave us here.

I suddenly want very much to be back in the bunk, making that plan with Riley, instead of having swung myself away from him. I've seen the inside of the Developer's workspace, so I know there are tools there. Tools that could get this disruptor off my head. It's four-against-one for Riley, but if I had the disruptor off, we might be able to take the bridge and make it out of here. We're more likely to win with those odds here than back in Kraysis-controlled space.

And in all solar hell, it's a better plan than waiting for them to leave us here.

It's at that moment I see One running up the tunnel. She runs like a military machine, all her movements economical. The change in g on the ship ramp has no effect on her pace, and she's barely breathing by the time she reaches us at the ramp head.

"Developer," she says, her eyes wide. "It's open."

9

The Developer runs just like One, which surprises me. For all his height and slenderness, the way he moves tells me he's been trained to fight. I mentally adjust the odds that Riley could best him, but mostly my thoughts are adrenaline sharp: *get down the tunnel.* I run all the way without noticing the change in g, and then I have to stop, disoriented, because the vault wall is no longer where it used to be.

The Developer pauses at this place, too. He is talking rapidly with One, so fast that I only catch enough words to know that Two and Three were still surveying the other tunnels when One noticed this breach in the wall.

Breach isn't quite what it is. A breach is a hole in something, a piece cut out or fragged out or vaporized, leaving a defect where once was whole. Here, the wall is simply gone, and the tunnel continues on into the dark moon rock. I have so many thoughts competing I can't follow any of them to a useful conclusion. That the Kraysis have left Riley alone on the ship. That the patterns in the dust seem different, but it's hard to tell with the Developer and One making prints. That the wall material must have gone somewhere, but where? That this might be the moment to run back to the ship. I decide that it is, just as I notice Two blocking retreat up the tunnel.

Instead, the Developer and One step across where the wall once stood, and I find myself following.

I smell a faint trace of cloves again. The Developer has some analyzer held into the air, probably to make sure we can still breathe. I take some comfort in him going first. If he falls over, I'll run.

But he doesn't and eventually the tunnel opens into a chamber where the temperature plummets. It's so cold I feel the heating grid in my suit kick in. In the doorway, the chamber roof is barely an arm-length over our heads, but the floor ahead is punched into a sunken circle. Facing down into that circle are three statues, who look very much like men in slimline spacesuits, stone helmets solemnly watching over the pit. And down in the pit are three dark spheres, about the size of a head, resting among drifts of blue-tinged ice.

My senses sharpen, remembering the spheres in that memory I pulled from the wall. Whoever made this place brought these spheres in and left them here. I look on them and see danger.

"Solid oxygen," the Developer says, pointing his analyzer at the ice. "Fascinating."

"I'd go for creepy," I whisper, thinking it looks like a tomb, especially with the statues. A cold tomb. Spheres buried in solid oxygen, on a moon with no geological activity, in a place that probably had no atmosphere until the Kraysis turned up. Seal upon seal upon seal. The wall was only one of them. The ice has a bare halo of sublimating gas, which probably explains the hyperalertness: there's extra oxygen in the air. The spheres have a mottled look about them, a dark stone laced through with something even darker and glassier, as the wall had been in the tunnel.

I can't shake the menace of those spheres, the worry I felt in that memory echo. They weren't sure they could contain it, even under all the seals. Maybe the statues were some final totem to ward off whatever it was.

The Developer seems to feel none of this. He's exuberant, making plans to send communications back, even as the cold soon pushes us out into the tunnel, and toward the ship. I pause when we pass where the wall used to stand and stare at the floor. The patterns in the dust reach all the way to our center tracks, as if the Developer and One made none when they walked around here less than an hour ago. But then the Developer has taken his light up the tunnel, and I can no longer see.

We meet Two near the end of the tunnel, who reports Three is still somewhere in the passages. The Developer orders them all back, so we can raise the ship to the top of the shaft to send a communication via the waygate relay. The disruptor clamps back on my head.

Riley is standing at the head of the ramp, his hands in his pockets. I wonder for a heartbeat if he's about to make a move, but he lets the Developer and One sweep past him, leaving the two of us alone at the ramp.

"They're taking off to send communications," I say. *Time to make that move?*

Riley shakes his head. "Didn't you notice the lights?"

"What lights?"

"The ship lights. How low they are in the main areas. And the grav-deck – it's running at lower g." He pauses. "That galley issue they've had for the past few clocks isn't isolated. They've got a power supply problem. I don't think we're going anywhere."

10

Riley turns out to be right. The Kraysis can't even power up the launch-start sequence. Even with the disruptor around my head, and sitting in our bunk, I can hear the whine of the acceleration loop trying to energize, and never making it. That shouldn't happen; the fusion drive should be powering it, with the battery cells evening out the supply. But it sounds like it's drawing on the battery cells alone.

Then, suddenly, the floor drops away. I lurch, taking a moment to realize we aren't actually falling. I look up and find Riley reeling from the shift, too. The gravity just made a big change. It feels like what used to happen whenever we stepped off the ship, which can only mean one thing.

"Grav-deck failure," Riley says.

We share the oh-shit stare without voicing it. A grav-deck failure can only mean the fusion drive is dead, which in the scale of problems from small to galactic, rates at least a heavy star. It's worse when you're a long way from help – say, across a blind river waygate at the edge of the 'verse.

And more: Three is missing. Riley and I overhear this from our lurking position outside the bunk door. We guess the Kraysis are thrown enough not to care what we're overhearing now. Three hasn't figured much in our time here – occasionally bringing the meals to the bunk, or standing in for One in applying the disruptor, but always available to any of the other Kraysis at a moment's call.

I have a bad feeling we've missed something.

Riley returns to the bunk, taking a portable screen and plugging it into a wall port.

I pause on my way out the door. "What are you doing?"

"They'll have to try re-starting the fusion drive. When they do, their network restarts as well. That's my way in. Where are you going?"

I don't answer. I figure I have a small window of time in the confusion. No one stops me as I grab one of the portable lights and shoot down the ramp. There's no change in g now. I throw up clouds of moon dust as I sprint into the tunnel. The first side passage is a blunt dead-end, and so is the second. After that, they become more branching. The floors all show the tracks of many boots passing through. It's on the fifth side passage, which actually runs deep into the moon, that I notice the floor. The moon dust has clearly been disrupted, a shallow path made with suspended material still in the air. But the lace-like vibration pattern has clearly reformed across the altered surface.

I stare at it, a manacle squeezing my chest. Admonishing myself for doubting Riley. We've definitely missed something.

I find Three in the next passage. I almost miss him, because he's no longer Three. His body has become part of the polished end wall, which is growing out tendrils along the rocky side of the tunnel. I take two steps back, my gaze fixed on the way Three's boots have become obsidian, like those statues inside the vault. The rest of his body is a smear of black, the advancing front of the material creeping visibly outwards. At the leading edge, it almost looks like a swarm of tiny maggots.

Well, giddy fuck.

I'm running again, back to the main tunnel, and like a rad-mad crazy person, back into the vault itself. I keep my feet on the moon dust, remembering that ancient vision the wall put into my head. They brought the spheres here, because it was cold. Because this moon was dead, and cold, and in a dying star system. They locked them behind a wall with a warning written in its fabric.

But maybe, even here, it wasn't cold enough.

The three statues are still there, but they seem slumped now, like wax in a warm room. More of the solid oxygen is gone, and those veins of black are visible through the floor now. And I think, fuck. Whatever this thing is, it's breached those spheres. Maybe it breached them long ago, using some tendril of geological heat from the moon, or the body heat of the three poor souls who stayed here to guard this pit of horrors. But that heat energy could only go so far.

Until the Kraysis brought a ship here with a fusion drive.

The low lights, the galley problem, the power supply issue … it all now makes sense, if you allow that some ancient *thing* has all this time been drawing energy out of the ship.

Every moment that I stood touching that wall, it was working on getting out. Hell, the puzzle of the signal in the wall was a great way to keep us here long enough to do just that. I suddenly feel unsure there was ever a lock to open; it could have just been the entity setting its trap. There are veins of it everywhere, through the rocks, probably all the way through the tunnels.

And if the Kraysis re-start that fusion drive, it will have more. *It will take the ship.*

The thought comes from the same place that ancient stone-memory lives, and I feel a chill through to my marrow. The Kraysis have unleashed an ancient thing here, something that destroys anything it touches, something that has been waiting cleverly for escape.

And I have helped it do that.

11

I pound on the bulkhead of the bridge until my hand turns red. "I found your comrade," I yell into the aerogel panel. "There's not much left of him."

When the Developer finally opens the door, One has a sidearm pointed at me, and behind her, Two has the ship's consoles open, a series of ceramic panels exposed. The telemetry screens are ominously dark.

I stare down One's weapon. "I advise you to point that another way."

"We have a problem with the ship," the Developer accuses. "Is this your doing?"

"You have a bigger problem. Whatever was in that vault is on its way out. I'm guessing it pulled so much energy out of the fusion drive that the reactor shut down."

The Developer has the grace to find a paler shade underneath his sweat-sheen. He takes a breath to speak, then stows the words, and instead tells Two to go and manually close the ramp.

After Two has left, he quietly says, "They told us it was dormant."

I have a feeling of this 'they' looming over us, whether it's some higher level of Kraysis society, or some kind of corporate who contracted the Developer. It all seems highly irrelevant now.

"Never seen a dormant thing smear a person to molecules," I say. "They also tell you it could suck the power out of a starship?"

"They suspected from the etchings it was a resonance material," the Developer says vaguely, as if trying to remember a briefing that seems too long ago. "Therefore remotely configurable at nanomechanical scale. I suppose … such a remote resonance capability might extend to power sources, if its field excitation was so flexible. This is … unexpected."

"I'd say it's fucked. We need to leave, before any of that black stuff makes it into the ship, if it hasn't already. And you need to take this thing off my head."

The Developer raises his hands slightly, as if the surface under his fingers might be contaminated. "The main power cell is empty. We cannot re-start the fusion drive."

"What about the auxiliary?"

He shakes his head.

This is not exactly what any ship's technician wants to hear. No power cells means no way to re-start a fusion drive. The kind of problem that has any normal ship pinging for a rescue. Only we can't even send a ping from down in this shaft, let alone keep that entity out for long enough to be rescued.

"Take this thing off my head," I say. "There's another way to re-start the drive."

But the Developer hesitates as if he's just catching up. "If this entity is a resonance power consumer … once we re-start the drive, we will only energize it further. If it is already mobile, then it may be unstoppable."

Through the lower clear panels of the bridge viewing ports, I catch a movement. Two is standing past the bottom end of the ramp, staring at something near the tunnel mouth.

"What is he looking at?" the Developer says.

"I'm not sure—" But I stop, because I see it. There's a face forming in the wall near the tunnel mouth, an actual goddamn face, its features slowly resolving in obsidian relief. A face that was obviously Three's.

I feel a cold like I'll never know warmth again.

"They tell you this stuff was capable of mimicry?" I say. "Take this fucking thing off my head."

The Developer's mouth hangs open, watching what happens next in paralyzed horror. Two steps across to the wall, peering at the face of his comrade. As he approaches, the pace of the face's construction noticeably quickens. I only have time to say, "Call him back," before Two reaches out, and then it's too late.

Two jerks his hand back, but the fingers are already turning black. He shakes the hand, like trying to throw off a spider, but the black is flowing into his shoulder. In two more heartbeats,

Two no longer exists, except as a black mass feeding off his body heat and flowing through the moon dust toward the ship.

I wrench the Developer up from his seat. "Take this fucking thing off!"

It's One who finally does it, and before the neural disruptor has hit the floor, I'm sliding down the bridge ladder, yelling for Riley as I run to the ramp. I figure we've got only minutes before we share the same fate.

12

Riley catches up to me at the head of the ramp, screen in hand. "The ship's main systems are dead," he says.

"Not yet," I say, as I throw the manual ramp retract handle around and around. "We need to re-start that fusion drive. We have to re-route the escape pod power cells to do it."

"Those cells aren't connected to the main network," he says. "I'd have to manually bridge the connection." But he's already stripping off his flight jacket and removing a panel on the far side of the cargo bar wall. "There's a crawlspace around the locked bulkhead here."

"Those cells being unconnected is the only thing saving us," I pant. The ramp is half retracted, but I can see that black mass through the tiny gap, still sliding through moon dust, striving for the ship. It's not moving across the dust; it's consuming it, gouging a trail as it goes. "But those pod cells are tiny. They'll be spent after one shot at a fusion re-start."

"And then?" Riley's already shouldering into the space.

"Immediate dust-off, maintaining the bridge connection to recharge those cells. We might need the escape pods."

Riley pauses. "So, we don't charge the main power cells?"

"No time." I keep throwing the handle around. Nearly there.

"Without those main power cells, some of the systems will be down. Like guidance. And stabilizing."

"I know," I say. "Don't wait. We needed to leave two clocks ago."

As Riley disappears, he says into my head, *I don't want to look out the window, do I?*

Tell me when that connection's made, I say. *Going back to the bridge.*

‹‹›››

I run my hands over the comms lines along the wall as I go, but its all eerie silent under my fingertips. Not a signal resonates in my head. There's not even residual buzz of a charge in the ship's lines. The black thing has taken all the energy.

The Developer is still in the bridge, peering out of the viewing ports. One hovers over the control panels.

"Get ready to re-start the drive," I say. Out the window, the black thing is close enough for its edge to be below the view. It could already be crawling up the landing strut.

"With what?" says One, but she flips open the cover and grips the fusion re-start handle.

I wait for Riley in my head.

"If you re-start the drive," the Developer says, "the entity will begin drawing the power again. Which will both limit the energy we can use, and speed its spread—"

Done, comes Riley's voice.

"Fire," I yell.

And bless One, she yanks that handle like a ripcord. I feel a shift, not in my head, but in the fizz of my blood. It comes from deep in the ship, an electric jolt of current surging in my senses. I feel it slam into the firing pins of the fusion drive, vibrations that are in my skin and nails and every cartilage cell in my body. At then, almost immediately, I feel that power evaporating, dancing out across space-time.

"*Solar hell*," I whisper, feeling the firing pins in the drive dropping their output.

I can't let this happen. The reactor isn't at critical mass yet, and if it fizzles, we are all dead. So I do the only thing I can: I feel for that power leak, for its resonance vibration, and I push back against it.

A force comes back against me like a cudgel, a colossal insidious power. I only hold a second before I have to let go, or it would have cored me out like worms on a corpse. I stagger up, heaving breaths. Was it enough?

"Drive re-start," yells One. "Re-start!"

Lights are coming back on across the screens, but even so I can feel a power drain itching through my senses. And there's a new creeping interference in the ship's systems when I put my hand to her walls. *It's already on board.* I know it.

"Dust-off, *now*," I say, as the grav-deck comes back online. I feel my spine compress under near-Earth g again.

"We don't have all systems up—"

"Now. That thing is already on the ship."

I turn to the Developer as the engines whine through start. "What's the range of your life boats?"

He blinks at me. The ship shudders as we lift off, lurching toward the side of the shaft. I grip the bulkhead as the grav-deck struggles to compensate, trying to steady our trajectory.

Through gritted teeth I say, "Can they get back to the waygate?"

"They need authority …" he starts.

I haul him up by the collar, helped by another lurch from the ship. "Why, did you think you weren't coming?" Then I turn back to One. "Clear us out of the shaft and then wedge the manual boost into orbit. Then run to the life boats. *Run.*"

〈〈 〉〉

The cancerous hum in the ship's systems accelerates as the Developer and I dodge the lurching toward the life boats. The lights dim as we go, then brighten, then dim again. We must be clear of the moon shaft by now, but without guidance, there's a risk the dynamics of the ship will destabilize, and the boost One is currently wedging on could send us sideways, or some other direction even less desirable. Our weight running around the ship won't be helping. I'm betting the entity could survive a crash. I'd bet more we would not.

I keep in front of the Developer, just in case he has any ideas of closing a bulkhead in my face. Riley is standing at the lifeboat rear-door entry, next to a wall panel where he's set the power bridge. He's ripped a gash down his cheek and another on his arm through the flight suit, but he's still a welcome sight.

"We seem to be flying," he says. "A little wild on the stick, but still."

As he says it, there's a sputter and a deceleration that makes me light on my feet. "Engines are down," I say. Now we're cruising on the First Law only, minus whatever the moon's gravity is sucking out of us. "Pull that bridge connection. The fusion drive's about to go down again. Ready the escape launch."

We need to clear the ship before that drive goes down.

Before the entity finds a way to pull power from the lifeboat power cells, too.

As Riley climbs into the pilot seat and the Developer sags into another, I sense One coming down the bridge ladder.

"Ready," I say.

One's steps are audible now. Thud, thud. Vibrations I feel through the floor and wall. She's tired. I stand in the door of the boat, waiting. My body is screaming to go, but you don't leave anyone behind. Not even a Kraysis.

"Steady."

One finally comes into view, staggers a step. The fusion drive collapses in that moment, and the grav-deck fails. It's suddenly dark, but for the light thrown down the hall from the escape pod. For half a heartbeat, I float, and so does One. And then, she's gone, and there's nothing but a crawling mass of black in the hallway.

"Go," I yell, and pound the door-closure. Its explosive bolt goes off as fast as the mortar round of grief and regret in my head. *Fuck this fucking fuck.*

Then the acceleration of the pod is merciful, knocking me to blackout.

13

The mercy only lasts heartbeats. I come round floating above the floor in the tight space behind the pod access door and the seats, feeling the thrum of the boost engine.

"We're shallow. Thirty percent." Riley's voice is in flat Special-Ops mode. He means our orbit, and our power cell. "Twenty. Shutting down."

The thrum silences as the engine dies. Into that silence, I strain my senses, feeling for that creeping interference in the pod, that maggoty wriggling vibration that I felt on the ship. It's not here. We may have just left the entity behind.

"Can you see it?" I say, careening into the co-flight seat and suppressing a wave of nausea. Haven't done zero-g in a long while.

Riley points to the console. There's two views on the cut-down displays: a screen showing orbital positions of nearby gravitational objects, and another plain camera view marked as 'rear'. The camera view is hard to read: the receding crescent of the red-lit moon, and a dark ship silhouette against it. There's a glint of the red on the ship's surfaces too, as if it's now mirror-polished obsidian.

The orbital grav-map is more definitive. The moon behind us, flagged as a heavy object, the ship with a minor tag. The waygate is marked and tagged too, out on our port and above the horizon. Way off our trajectory.

"Do we have enough power to correct?" I ask.

Riley doesn't answer. He's still staring at the orbital positions on the grav-map. "Just, I think," he says finally. "But … that ship is moving."

I stare at the Kraysis ship we just left behind, and in solar hell, he's right. It isn't just moving, it's maneuvering. And I don't need Riley to do a course prediction to know it's heading for the waygate.

In that instant, I have a vision of what it could mean if that ship passes through the waygate and back into the inner systems. Where the entity could feed on a million fusion drives, both space-side and planet-side, transforming matter all the way back to Earth.

I turn to the Developer, who's also staring at the grav-map screen. "Tell me that your ship can't just pass through."

He takes a breath, and in his hesitation, I already have the answer. "These life boats require authorization. But our main ship broadcasts with encrypted permission that our waygates automatically detect."

"Correct our course," I say, strapping into the seat. "We can't let it through the waygate."

"No," he says softly.

We sit there in zero-g silence, strapped to our seats as Riley burns the course correction and reads the diminishing power charge as he does.

"Fifteen percent. Ten. Five."

I watch the trajectory line come around with want-to-scream slowness, until finally our course lines up with the waygate and Riley shuts it down.

"Three percent remaining," he says.

"Three percent," I echo, looking at the intercept line on the entity's ship. We'll get there before they do, courtesy of the small head-start, but not much before. In that moment, while I'm applying my mind to the problem, a sensation like a roll of g-forces tumbles through me. I hear my own gasp before it passes. Weird.

"What?" Riley says.

"Nothing," I say, as Riley gives me a hard look. "So we've three percent to work out how to get through the gate, and then close it down behind us."

Everyone is silent, because we're on a lifeboat. We don't have weapons here. We just have me, a neural-grafted ship's doctor, an ex-Special Ops man, and a Kraysis technologist. Three soft, breakable bodies, and three percent power.

"We cannot close it down," the Developer says.

I look down at the floor. "Well, here's the options. Either we work out how to do it, or we spend our three percent charting a crash course for the gate's control hub, because we aren't letting that ship through."

And that fairly shuts him up.

14

A waygate, as that old physicist would have pointed out, is a field device. It shares an entangled space-field with its twin gate, and it uses its power source to excite the shared field so that they momentarily touch each other in space-time. The details are ludicrously technical. But we don't have time for technical. The distance is closing fast.

We've already talked about bomb making, for which we have no materials, and making a bolide from the pod's jettisonable engine, which is sure to fail. But the power is a critical system for the gate, and our engine is one of the few tools we have, so we keep circling back.

"If we jettisoned the engine behind us, it could strike the ship," the Developer says, but he sounds hopeful, like a child who wishes he didn't know anything about orbital dynamics.

"More likely it will sail right past. Or they will avoid it. Or even if it hits, this entity will just consume it, too. What about accessing the waygate control system, and shutting down its power source?"

The Developer quietens again as we all feel a pre-jump bounce, which makes my blood fizz. As if it wasn't fizzing already with the possibility of unleashing an all-consuming entity on the populated systems, a situation I am party to bringing about.

Riley has been busy all this time, interfacing with the waygate's protocols on the screens.

"We don't have any time to hack the system," he says quietly. "It's a hardened interface. That would take a clock's worth of trying, even if I was on board the thing and wired in directly. The only thing I've been able to get is a list of standard operating rules."

We all fall silent, feeling the ticks of the seconds like hull breaches, each saying this is the end of the line, and this pod is the last place we'll know in the 'verse.

I stare at the screens, then at the gate looming very large in the window. Something about what Riley's done bothers me.

"Wait, how are you even able to talk to the gate? Didn't the Developer say these pods required authorization?"

The Developer hitches a breath, as if he's just realized a mistake. "Authorization was required on the near-side of the gate—"

Then I realize. "But this end was sailing through interstellar space for decades. No one programs authorization that far in advance. It would risk locking themselves out of the gate at this end. Expensive mistake."

"It's an older gate, not upgraded," Riley says, slowly. Then he dives back into the protocols, furiously searching. A moment later, he sits back, stabbing a finger at the screen. "There's two rules we can use."

"One transmission per cycle," the Developer says, reading off the screen.

Riley nods. "The gate only powers the field for the moments it's needed. And then it takes some time to recharge the capacitance from its fusion drive. You wouldn't want the field cutting off when a ship was half-way through, so it only allows one at a time. Newer gates have big capacitors and allow a certain passage window, but older ones were conservative. Even older Kraysis gates. In the inner systems, older gates were upgraded, but not this one."

The Developer purses his lips. "All gates are Kraysis gates."

Party-line to the end.

I look at our trajectory converging with the entity ship. Close, very close. "So what if the ship has to wait a recharge cycle? That won't stop it."

"I said two rules. The gate also doesn't allow debris near its field. It's a failsafe against a disaster in a transmission being visited on the next ship, too. If there's debris detected, the gate requires active re-start from the other side. Gives them time to assess what's happened I guess."

"So you want to jettison the engine."

He nods. "If we purge it in the right place, it will contaminate the gate field, and the waygate will shut down until it has re-start command from the other side, long enough for our friend here to contact his people and make sure that doesn't happen. Or better yet, a self-destruct."

"The jettison would have to be calculated precisely for our orbit and angular velocity," the Developer says. "Otherwise it could fail entirely, or pass out of the gate field too soon to prompt a shutdown."

Riley is working furiously at his screen. "What do you think I'm doing here?"

So that is how the next clock-fractions go: Riley, written-in-the-marrow Kraysis hater, running calculations alongside the Developer. Checking each other and rechecking, until they have the timings down to the fractional second. It involves a complex roll maneuver to ensure the engine eject counters our velocity, allowing it to hover in the gate's field space, while ensuring we won't collide with it on our way through. All the while, the entity ship is closing on the waygate and us, and the pre-jump bounces are coming in pairs.

When everything is ready, Riley speaks into my head. *We're going to be drifting on the other side. No engine. We maybe enough power to make one distress call.*

I add, *and hope they will actually disable the gate.*

And all we can do is stare at each other and accept that those are the odds.

Finally, when the waygate's red-lit oval aperture is so large in the window all we can see is part of its rim, Riley begins the countdown.

"Ready to jump. In ten …"

I think about how they must have trained him to sound calm like that, and wonder if the calm goes all the way down into his soul, or if it's just the ice crust on a raging river.

"Nine, eight, seven, six …"

I hope there's a chance to find out.

"Five, four, three, two …"

Then there's the last shaking bounce. With it comes that tumbling weird g-force feeling again, and this time I know that something isn't entirely right with me, something that isn't to do with escaping this situation. Anesthetic white-out ends the thought. I'm barely aware of another jolt, which I think must be the engine eject, but it's muffled and distant to my senses, the way that memory in the vault wall was distant to whoever made it. The way many of my own are such a long way from me.

And then I see space again, with no more red-sun light, but a twinkling starfield, like the one I was watching from the viewing port many clocks before all this started.

15

We drift for a quarter clock past the waygate before a Kraysis ship shows on the grav-map screen. And not the obsidian one we've left behind either; it's one that heard our distress call.

I'm not sure it's much better for us.

The Developer's mood transforms. He's tense and distant, loosing any comradery might have just developed between us. I don't know what kind of penalties there are for having lost a ship, or what the circumstances were of this mission, but at least he's going home, and with a story to tell. From the chatter between him and the ship, the waygate is being locked out, and who knows how many committees and disciplinary processes that will generate. The Kraysis might be a walled-off, secretive people, but I'll bet all my currency they're as bureaucratic as Earth-central.

But common as bureaucracy might be, for us, the Kraysis are enemy territory. We are all exhausted, hungry, and strung out, a weak position. I imagine being disappeared into Kraysis space for all the cycles I have left.

"When we dock, you need to organize for us to be taken to the nearest Earth-central transfer station," I say, as soon as the Developer is off the channel with the intercepting ship.

He frowns. "We don't interact with Earth-central systems."

"Except when conducting espionage."

He has nothing to say to that.

"Or," I say, "provide us with a transport and we'll take ourselves there. We have done more than was asked of us, and more than we should have done given what's happened. There's a lot of shit to clean up, and we don't want any part in it."

Saying this denies the responsibility I feel, but as far as the Developer can know, I'm done with heroics. He needs to think this is on the Kraysis.

"Beyond that, we saved your ass," Riley says. "When we could have left you there with your comrades."

The Developer rubs at his nose. He seems unhappy. "They will not want loose ends, and I will not be able to sway them, especially over you. Our culture doesn't permit neural grafting. We don't modify our bodies, and committees are suspicious of anyone from the central systems who does."

There's a beat of silence, watching the approach of the Kraysis ship. It's a long, slender thing with dart-like engines in the back, large enough for three docks in the side. I have such a rage in me now. It took so long to break free of the systems that made me, and longer still to find this return-to-Earth plan with Riley. I will not be a captive again, and I start to wonder what lengths I will go to for that ship out there to not be a prison, when the Developer suddenly says,

"They will not allow you on board without a neural disruptor."

His tone is conspiratorial, an inflection I've not heard from him before.

"Really," I say, carefully.

"Yes. But I have worked much with neural disruptors these last clocks. As you know, they can enhance rather than restrict. But to a casual observer, one looks the same as another."

I share a glance with Riley.

"There will be time," he says, "when they are preparing the hearings, for all kinds of processes to go not quite to plan. Especially for one such as you."

"Why would you help us?" Riley says, as I try not to feel the surge of hope at the path of our escape.

"For all the reasons you have just relayed," he says quickly. "And several others, which perhaps Coryn Astridottir may remember in time."

As we spend our last moments here in the lifeboat, I feel the twitching tail of that memory that isn't quite allowing itself to surface. Of a favor done, or owed, or some other kindness that is so tied into the parts I've forgotten it won't allow itself to emerge. There is too much more pressing in the current moment: ancient entities threatening to walk through a waygate into the central systems. An enemy ship to navigate. An escape to make. A start-over plan to start-over.

"Thank you," I say, and I mean it not for this help he is gifting now, but for whatever past thread it is we have together, that's woven into the patched and mended fabric I am now.

He ghosts a smile. *And maybe we will meet again*, he says into my head.

Afterword

Hey there, you made it to the end. That's a great thing — as a writer, it's always a milestone. As a reader, it might mean you liked it, or at least, you were belligerent enough to stick with it if you didn't.

So, now you're here, I'm going to do the annoying bit where I ask you to help me earn a living. You already paid for the book, awesome, but now you can leave a review where you bought it. Reviews show that a title is being read and help other readers to make better choices for books that will suit them. I believe in honest reviews, so have at it, and receive my grateful thanks for keeping me in paper and pencils.

And if you did enjoy this, you might like the previous two stories in the ship's doctor saga – "The Ship's Doctor" and "Dellinger" – they follow here as a bonus in this print edition.

— Charlie, September 2020

The Ship's Doctor

Adventures of Coryn Astridottir #1

This is the way it always ends.

My cheek burns from his stubble and blood rushes to my head. Got up too fast, but we're five minutes from port. I grope for my trousers under the covers. They're crunched down below the bed end, inside-out, cast off in a rush. I turn them by feel, then go after my shirt. *Be gone before he's back.*

I hear him cleaning up through the thin bathroom walls. He was good, this one, with his reactor-ore-etched nails and whip scars on his back. From the prisons or military chain-gangs maybe. I didn't ask his name. I never ask. Once my need is gone, it's gone. Then, I can let the other desire take over.

I can remember who I am.

I put a hand to the pod wall, cold from the space-soak. Two engines push us towards port: one a DM-starrunner, the other a MaximII. Their vibration thrills me, sending shivers dancing in my skin, a smile on my lips.

I interpret them while I pull on my trousers one-handed. The Maxim lags the DM, thrumming out of sync. Probably a coolant blockage. Nothing much fancy happens in the old gear. The pulse drive won't get much further than the return leg but it's not my concern. Some sap in the control room will see a red blinking light: this boat's only a red-class star freighter. A fast shuttle. I'll forget her before I've passed the airlock, just like the man in the bathroom. I never bothered to learn their names, because out there is the *Freya*. A blue-class mega station. Black shimmering crystal looming in the darkness.

After that, there's nothing else.

‹‹ ›

"Doctor."

A curt nod in khakis greets me at the entry dock. Stars on his shoulder say he's a second-captain, *Gibbon* stitched in white on his chest. Gibbon is a type of monkey, but I don't make the comment. It wouldn't help. Gibbon's a man whose humor evaporated into space years ago.

So I nod in return, take his hand firmly. "Captain."

He pauses just a bit too long. I know what he sees. Young woman. Too young. Too pink. Too pretty. But I forgive him that. He doesn't know. He licks sweat from his upper lip. The *Freya* is a big deal when you don't trust the physician. And he's old enough to think it's all bunk. Doctors for ships, new-verse crap.

No sense in jerking around.

"What is the nature of your problem, Captain?"

Gibbon's eyes flash left and right.

"Not here," he murmurs with a nervous glance to the crowds in the dock.

He turns on his heel and we're walking to *Freya*'s hub, waved through border control, on the long journey to the control deck. The *Freya* is the size of a planet-side city, like suburbs stacked one on another. She's a parasite station, hanging above Artemis, whose blue oceans are the only reminder of home. The Artemis system's the frontier of transformed worlds and *Freya* is the gateway. Space elevator. Captured asteroid miner. Terraformer. Bolt hole. My heels flash at the disgruntled crowds lining up with passports. I meld into the noise, following my monkey. They don't even scan my case.

The lift is a bullet in a tube, doors marked in red *Authorized Only*. Gibbon's fingertip glows with a red LED beneath his skin as his touch grants access. My desire stirs then; I want to touch it, feel the machine in the man, just as I itch to touch the walls and feel Freya's pulse. But Gibbon's a tense sort and there'll be time enough for astonishment. I am beginning to feel her anyway. Men like Gibbon barely appreciate what's in these walls. A new kind of thing entirely.

Two red bullets later, a blue-striped door declares *Operations*. Gibbon announces me, scuttles off. I've unsettled him and he doesn't know why, never will. Good for him.

The council of eight first-captains stands in a clutch. More khakis with loops of red at the shoulder. Ex-military men tending a sick giant. Giddy hens in a circle. The one with the extra gold bars steps forward.

"Doctor," he says with an inflection I don't like. His name is Murphy. I want to make a joke about the irony, but I don't. That part of my brain still works, but it's under control these days. Murphy introduces the others. I slide my eyes past their faces, not remembering names.

"What is the nature of your problem, Captains?" I press.

Murphy shifts in his shoes.

"First of all, I need to impress—"

I want to hiss. He thinks of legality and his ass before the station. I glance at his pants. No, not even an ass worth saving. But it's not him at stake. I give him a clinical smile, reassurance, no humor.

"Doctor-patient confidentiality was extended in the last verse approved regs, Captain. Don't worry, you're covered."

He breathes out.

"The core is fluctuating," he volunteers. *What the fuck do we know, you're the doc...*

I put down my case and turn to the wall screens.

"Bring me up the vitals, please."

A hovering tech engineer glides forward to man the controls. The old men don't get themselves dirty on the keys. Likely never learned to type. I'd do it myself, but I think faster this way. And I have to go through the motions, not to scare them first, and to let my connection find its frequency.

The tech's fingers dance. Data readouts fill the main screen, another scrolls graphs tagged in multicolored Helvetica. Colors grow and shift. No one in the room can read it; proprietary design. Nothing trips my pattern recognition, so I start on The List. I pine for direct connection, but I'm not there yet. My brain takes a while to scan the frequencies.

"Primary line pressure?" I begin.

I don't like this part; makes it seem like she's a machine, no respect for what she really is. I'm not a mechanic. But it does give the onlookers some comfort.

"Twenty bar median, ranging eighteen to twenty-point-five," answers the Tech.

His voice is calm, deep. Not bored. I like that. *Careful.* I keep my eyes on the screen.

"Normal then. Core field?" I continue.

"Half Tesla."

"Holding steady?"

"Blips two percent on a four-hour-cycle," he offers, matter-of-fact, professional.

I grunt. Unusual to get that sort of variation. I cast an eye at the techie's pocket. *Riley.* Strong hands. My brain drags my eyes upwards. Strong jawline too. *Please, not when I'm working.*

His eyes, an odd deep red, flicker to mine. He looks away quickly, with a small frown. Like he did something wrong. He avoids looking up again. His cheeks burn red like his eyes. He clears his throat.

"We changed out five filters in the last planet-cycle," he volunteers, staring at the wall.

"And?"

He licks his lips.

"And what, ma'am?"

"Why did you change them?"

He flushes. "The red light went on."

I nearly double take. No one goes by instrument panel anymore. But then I remember where I am. The furthest flung blue-class in the known verse.

"I need to see those filters," I say.

"Uh… they went to the recyclers."

I turn to stare at the first-captains.

"Gentlemen. You cannot destroy specimens. And you cannot put unchecked parts into the recyclers. This isn't a mechanical works, with parts that *break* and get *replaced.* She's a grafted organism."

"It's standard procedure—"

"I don't give a damn."

It snaps out of me, curt. Murphy shuts his jaw, squashing his cheeks.

"How long have these fluctuations been going on?"

"Forty planet cycles, give or take," says Riley.

"How long is that here?"

"About two Earth weeks."

"Two weeks?"

I glare at them. Dammit. They'd let her go for two weeks. The information brings a memory I don't want: of hot raw burn to my sinuses. I suck cooling air through my nose to forget.

"It took half that time getting you here," complains Murphy. "Anyway, I don't see the problem. There's a leak somewhere, a processor down, whatever. We haven't lost critical systems—"

"*Time* is precisely the nature of your problem," I snap, mind doing the math. *Gods, two weeks!* "This isn't a leak, captain. A station this size can't maintain critical systems for two weeks on a leak."

I've folded my arms. My toe taps. I picked that up from my registrar at the docks and I've never shaken it. He even spoke to the ships that way. Time to take control.

"Riley, I'm going to need a sample."

"You going to explain what you're doing?" Murphy tries to re-establish authority. The other first-caps nudge each other, all that powder gray precision suddenly not delivering.

But I wasn't, not yet. They'd have their answers. But sharing information now will slow me down. I don't blame them; they're fearful. They remember the *Selenium*. She died spiraling into a sun, when the DNA microsplice tech was new. We all remembered her, because her doc went down with her. There were rumors about why. But this wasn't about that, not exactly. Riley and I have a date with *Freya*.

❬❭❭

Riley keeps quiet at first. He walks beside me, along cleated maintenance deck grateways, a system the passengers never see. His manners change. Back straighter. Jaw set. He's not as green as I thought, just a show for the ops room. If someone had asked, he'd have said he was leading me to the core system hatches, but no one leads me anywhere on a ship. I could have followed her heart with my hand on the walls.

"So, what do you need a sample of?"

We stop at a bullet call point. Riley's thigh is long and muscled under the blue fatigues, which run a smooth line from belt to knee. *Not now.* I look at his face instead. Unlined, earnest. Interested. *Damn.*

"What do you know about the core?"

"Blue-class StarLiner Evo model," he says, like the fine print from the catalogue. His red eyes shine.

I pause.

"Not many people know that."

"Know what?" he asks. I wait as the bullet slides open and we step inside. The doors close.

"That the station's core defines its class, not its size," I say.

"Oh. My dad—"

He catches himself as the bullet whizzes away. My stomach drops before the magnos kick against the acceleration. My grandmother knew the man who developed the magnos. That still gives me a rush.

"What else do you know?" My eyes wander to his buttocks. They curve under the blue drill, muscled and hard as a synthetic melon. He catches me looking.

"Its proprietary… some of the guys in tech wanted to take one apart, see what was in there, but it's not supposed to be a good idea."

"That's right. Know why?" The bullet accelerates again.

"Because it's a living machine," he says softly.

"That's right." I close my eyes, put a hand on the wall. *A living machine.*

The exact details are secret, of course, but that doesn't mean I don't know. The Company spliced DNA programs with the micromachines in the core, programs that could copy themselves, evolve, be selected, multiply. Superior to anything they'd ever programmed in software. That made it possible to make a system for a blue-class that wouldn't be obsolete as soon as it left the dock. The hitches were years in development, but they were mostly about getting the signal out. No one had built ports for something that was living matter on a scaffold.

In the end, it didn't matter. In a few generations, the DNA machines built their own scaffolding onto microwires, massive bandwidth, parallel processing. But then the techs couldn't understand what went on inside. It didn't look like what they'd programmed anymore. They couldn't diagnose the problems.

Then they found out they didn't have to, not exactly. All they needed were us.

The ships' doctors.

《〈〉》

We leave the bullet at the core deck. Riley swipes a glowing LED finger over the reader. I'm having a hard time keeping my attention off him. The strength in his hands, the stamina of a youthful body. Only the core room lets me forget for a while.

I put my case on the floor and pull it open. An old-style doctor's case with pouches, slots and hidden places. It smells of leather and Listerine. I get my tools. Fifty mil syringe and sixteen gauge needle in plastic packets. Swab and graft plaster. Gloves, goggles. Mask. I hold one out to Riley, which he takes with a confused expression.

"What do I need that for?"

"Because you wouldn't want to be sorry."

He shrugs and pulls it on. Obedient too. *Probably looks good in leather.* The urge is getting a long-nailed hold. I shake my head, trying to dislodge it.

I go to the walls then: thousands of four-inch square panels with quarter-turn fasteners holding them over the central exchange. From here, *Freya* sends her nervous system all over the station, even grows satellite control centers where they're needed. But this, right here, is the master.

I listen through my fingertips and finally I feel her frequencies resolve under my touch. My heart skips to beat in time with her, and the connection rush squashes my other urge. Our minds, such as hers is, speak. Our direct connection is nearly complete. And I feel her system choking. I follow the stress to a high point, then point to the panel.

"Here."

Riley gets his quarter-turn tool. I unwrap the syringe, tip it with the needle. He turns the four points with a practiced hand and the small window to *Freya*'s core stands open.

❬❬❭❭

At first, it looks like a jumble. A gelatinous web, like jellyfish running with pale blue streams piled one on another: oxygen dissolved in inorganic medium. The look of it isn't right, but it wasn't what I was hoping for. On *Selenium* the microwires got an impurity and corroded. The sloughing debris poisoned the DNA and the whole system went down. Making calculations while sick and a-kilter, she ran into a sun, my colleague still trying to stabilize the poison. But if the wires were corroding, there should be rivers of red or black shot through the mix.

This is something else. Distributed, cloudy. I tell myself it's no big deal, but I still bite my lip, remembering. Because there was another station before the *Selenium*. One that never made it out of port.

One that got infected.

❬❬❭❭

My breath steams my goggles as I plunge the needle tip into the cloudy goo. It's only ten mil under the thin membrane. My thumb moves the plunger by muscle memory, and a thick spurt of pale blue sits in the barrel. I withdraw, swab the spot and stick on the graft plaster. Riley has the panel on before I've capped the needle.

"Now what?" he asks.

"Analysis."

"And you're expecting what?"

He leans over me as I pull the mobile micro-bio unit from my bag. I try to ignore him, running a loving finger along the keypad. It's crude, limited range of species, but accurate. I load the sample cassette, click it home. The red light blinks, working.

I look up at Riley then. His hair – the color of burnt umber – touches his skin like fronds of a willow hiding one strange eye. My hand moves to his leg.

The unit's light blinks green before I get there, and I turn the move into asking for a hand up. Riley obliges, grip firm and sure. My urge flutters uncomfortably, and I do what I never do. I hold his eye with mine.

"What does it say?" he whispers, breath hot and close.

《〈〉》

"You have an infection."

The first-captains stare at me. One moves his mouth like a fish.

"I'm sorry, what?"

"You have an infection. *Pseudomonas astrolix* and *Radiosolis* virus."

Bugs born in the gamma radiation-soaked cold space, so far departed from Earth species it's like they never saw planet-side at all.

Murphy scratches at his armpit, beetroot fingers deep within starched khakis. Looks like he gets along with Gibbon.

Someone at the back pipes up.

"Is that a software virus?"

"Can they even get infected?" Their voices flutter into a rabble.

And Murphy comes to where I want him: impatience.

"Alright, ok. Infection. What do we do? Is it serious?"

I breathe out. Once they start asking for advice, usually things go smoothly. I melt a little.

"Can be, but you're fortunate. These cores have an immune system, too. She actually fights pathogens all the time. This infection's a bit more serious, but I'll find a suitable course of anti-viral and anti-microbe. Order it on the next fast shuttle. We'll shut down to critical systems. You don't want to maneuver. She'll recover."

I look around their faces. Relief, boredom, acceptance. House of monkeys.

I press forward.

"You know, this is pretty straightforward stuff. If you had a resident doc, you'd have had it sorted out a week ago."

At this, Murphy's face squashes into a disgruntled humph.

"We did," he grunts. "He died, that's why you're here."

Something wicked claws my innards. It feels like freefalling to planet-side, turning inside-out, drifting in space without a suit.

"When?" My voice is a knife, sharp, fearful. *Please no …*

Murphy shrugs.

"Just on an earth week ago. Space fever. Died in his bunk."

I hiss involuntarily. My teeth chill from the air rush. *"In his bunk?"*

"What?"

I force myself to be calm, pleasant. Make him forget the hiss. As pleasant as I can get. Space fever. Code for infection.

"Captain, order the station to quarantine."

"What? Why?" demands Murphy.

"Do it! I'll be back in an hour."

I grab Riley by the collar. "Take me to the doctor's bunk," I hiss.

〈〈〉〉

The doctor's bunk is cramped and cluttered with journal papers and yellowing texts in piles and spilling from suitcases. I run my fingers across the crumbling sheets; not many use paper anymore. Dirty cups and a crumb-speckled plate sit atop the stacks on the tiny desk. Twisted-nail and holographic puzzles cluster in rows on a high shelf. Regs say the crew must wait a fortnight before they can dispose of his gear. That might save the station yet. The bed is still rumpled. A touch screen blinks idle over the bed.

"I need his notes. He would have recorded all he did."

I touch the screen but it asks for a print-scan and password. I swear at my lack of implants.

Riley moves close, his fingers replacing mine.

He glances sidelong as the system screen glows in our faces.

"We could have done this from operations," says Riley. The screen reflects in his eyes.

"No, not this. Records are confidential. Can't be stored on the central system. Has to be here."

Riley's hands move deftly, opening the personal folders, bringing up screen after black screen. From the side, those strange red eyes brim like red caramel. I wonder if he has grafts. But just the thought brings excitement and I look away.

"Nothing. It's empty."

"It has to be there. He would have recorded something like this."

He checks again. I feel the block between me and the system, an agonizing distance. I long to jack in but I've never allowed myself the hardware. I don't think I could stop.

Then I look around me.

"Riley. Stop."

"What?"

"It's not in there."

I begin on the stacks of papers. *Of course.* All the ship's docs have a problem with machine fascination. Some think it's because we want to get inside our patients. But it's more than that. It's addiction. The way your heart skips when you control something this big. The way the universe expands in hard-wire connection. And more, we all knew how much it could bring us unstuck. Unable to do our jobs. Useless. We took measures. This doc kept his hands off the machines even for records. My problem, my insistent urge, is a little shade different, but not much.

Riley thumbs through piles alongside me, the cabin keeping us close. I hold my breath because he smells of spice and machine oil and the round muscle of his shoulder shows through his shirt as he reaches under my arm. He comes up with a fat leather-bound notebook, pages edged in grime.

I take the book, breathing in grease and sterilizer, anchoring myself back in the realm of doctoring. I flip to the last entry logs, half-way through the pages. I read it under my breath.

Drive continues in flux. Edema in capillary supply lines. Suspect pathogen. Sample analyzer requiring part. Aspirate sent fast pulse to Poseidon.

"So?" asks Riley.

"He did the same thing. But the on-station analyzer's broken. He sent the sample on a fast shuttle to Poseidon. He wouldn't have dared start a treatment without the sensitivity analysis. This could be good news; we'll have that earlier than I thought..."

But he'd died. And there's something not right about that. My eyes scan higher. I flip back a page, past the station's early clinical signs. Then, I find another entry. I feel cold writhe in my skin.

I point to the date.

"When was this?"

Riley tilts the book, eyes narrowed.

"Um, two weeks ago. Just after the last supply boat."

"When was the next one?"

"It was today – your boat."

I hiss, the sound rising from beneath my soul.

I drop the log, and it falls open at the entry: *Last order not sent. Reordered masks.*

Riley meets my eyes. His pupils contract, understanding.

"He took a sample," he says slowly. "But he was out of masks."

"First rule: no mask, no sample. Not when you might aerosolize an infection, breathe it right into your lungs…" I speak right from the handbook, that first week in the docks.

Then the comms buzz Riley's tracer; it comes through on the overhead speaker.

"Doctor. We have an issue in med dock. I'd like you back in operations… please."

It's Murphy. About to learn his law.

With the station in lock-down, all door readers are set to red, but Riley's micromesh fingertip is customized to *allow*. We glide seamlessly through empty corridors, feet falling in step. There's urgency, doubled by my compulsion, which is starting to assert itself again. I curse it, but it's there. And I feel the pressure of company as soon as we're inside operations. Then I know I'm not going to be able to put it aside. It will grow until *Freya* is only at the edge of my mind, unable to perform my function, victim to my failing. And that's the only thing that's worse than the urge itself.

Murphy quilts his jaw while the other captains sit around the low table, crumpled gray faces above crumpled shirts. Riley is bright and fresh in the corner of my eye. I clench my teeth, holding onto focus.

"How many cases do you have, Captain?"

Murphy shifts in his seat.

"Four."

"Who are they?"

"Two émigrés serving waiting times, staying near the doc's room. And a cook, and a cleaner."

"Shit." I say it out loud. I never got the pre-processor implant, the one that lets you review messages sent to the speech center before they go out. I suspect Murphy has one. Right now, he probably wishes I did too. But a cook and a cleaner see dozens of people every day. If the station had infected the doc, the doc had infected the station.

To his credit, Murphy only raises a caterpillar eyebrow.

"How long till it spreads? What do we do?"

I sigh, allowing him to feel a little weight of the issue. But I try not to think of *spreads*.

"Seems a week for incubation. There's nothing to do. Stay in lock-down. The sample was sent, we have to wait for the sensitivity. You have a doc in the med lab?"

A *real* doc, that is. Murphy nods.

"Let him handle it. Alone. Minimize contacts. I'll handle the station. Go back to your quarters. The fast shuttle will have the answer here as soon as they can. I will monitor *Freya* with Officer Riley."

The captains are caught uncomfortable needing to take direction from another and there's a lull. But I've seen this before. It's quick, and then comes relief: doing *something* that feels so easy, much like doing *nothing*. They leave, a flotilla of military walks, stodged with age, emptying the halls and into the bullets. Riley turns his back to follow them.

I wait.

He glances back as he walks, a smile on his lips, red blush creeping down his cheekbones. I take just the moment to watch the hall, feeling *Freya* turn around us, her sickened soul filling the walls. The sensation blooms to full perception just then: I've made full connection. Blood rushes to my head and my lips tingle, like a moment in freefall, pure thrill.

And at least she's stable. Because now, the need is upon me, strong and unyielding. So, when Riley turns unhurried at the end of the hall, I follow.

This is the way it goes.

❮❮❯❯

Riley's room is a standard issue gray-walled serviced cabin. The air is dry, with a faint musk that disguises the usual bouquet of cleaning chemicals from the bathroom.

He holds open the door. On the low shelves, a squat glass bottle is the origin of his smell; it's on his clothes, even on the rough blankets made to military precision on the bed. The small table holds a pile of yellowing paperbacks next to a wireless tablet, like a Zen garden. Uniforms, pressed and crisp, fill the slim tall cupboard, jeans and shirts stuffed on the shelves below. A digital frame on the wall scrolls photos; heavy military freighters in dock, Riley in civvies with a tall man, a bikini model I recognize from Poseidon. Two lives in the same cabin.

Riley presses the door closed and locks it with his fingertip. My pulse quickens at the glow under his skin, and the flash of his eyes as the light catches the edge of the grafts. He leans against the door.

"Nice place." I speak only to cut the air. Too much tension, it will be over too fast. He looks at me steadily.

"I've never met a woman like you before," he says, the blush creeping a little lower. He can't quite meet my eyes.

I tilt my head very slightly. "No, you haven't."

The cabin is small, we are very close. The scent of him grows stronger. I step forward. The low light glints off his red-blond stubble. We stand an inch apart. The air heats between us. His eyelashes dip as he glances down. His pupils expand so they become red rims, then contract to pinpricks as I cast a shadow on his face. *Nice.*

"Who did your eyes?"

"I don't remember."

"Fed forces?"

He doesn't answer but taps finger to thumb; the lights fade. I sense myself in green afterglow on his retinas. Those aren't passive grafts. They're clever parts with an AI that demands a link-up. My brain doesn't have a gate in that circuit and I can't turn off. Built to bond to hybrid systems. Men and their machines.

Our left fingers brush together and his right hand cups my head, tilting. I feel the connecting electro-nerve pulse sparkle. But I'm in long before he is. I brace, my fingers hook his back and I jack his mind through those eyes.

❮❬❭❯

It is over, but he doesn't leave.

I lie in the crook of his arm, all heated skin. His fingers play idly on my shoulder.

"How old are you?" he asks.

I smile in the dark. *Freya* beats in the wall behind me, tiny pulses in her supply capillaries matching Riley's heartbeat.

"Old enough," I say.

He strokes my neck. He takes a breath to say something. Stops, and doesn't. Raises the lights just a fraction.

"Star Ops," he says finally. "My eyes."

I nod in the dim, looking up. His irises give a slight rainbow shimmer as he shifts from infrared back to light spectrum. It's a good job; the early grafts had no control, infrared all the time. I tell him so. He knows. Says his dad knew people.

"You don't have any machine splices. No implants, hybrids?" he asks softly.

"No. It's best I don't. I couldn't stop."

I sense him frown.

"Odd for a ship's doc. But you're not a clean slate, are you? What do you have?"

Perceptive. Have to be for Star Ops.

"Not implants," I say quickly. "Transplant. Autologous."

"What is that?"

I stifle a sigh. I am released now, and *Freya's* presence sits heavy in my mind. Her cells vibrate with mine, like strings of one instrument. She is sluggish, but though nothing has changed with her, I don't like to linger. It is not for me.

I go to get up, but his hand closes on my arm. My hair tumbles around my face; its touch is odd, something I almost never feel.

"I want to understand," he says.

I try to shake him off, but he is persistent. Lapse of my judgment, I can usually avoid the inquisitive ones.

"Please," he presses. Asking, not begging.

I look him right in the eye. And my transplant finishes its connection to his graft. *Dammit.*

"A long time ago, when the techs were new—" I begin.

"In a galaxy far, far away?" he asks with a grin.

I stop, unsmiling. To his credit, he lets the grin fall. I'm not a roll to joke with.

We stare at each other, his grafted eyes glimmering. From our wireless connection, I see the image of me in his mind: pearly skin, with dark eyes he thinks are sucking at his soul. Genuine regret, genuine interest. I stop pulling against his arm.

"If I wanted to be a ship's doc like you, what would I need to do?" he asks softly.

I remember steel and a clean smell. Long ago. No time for the details.

"Have your neurons harvested. Then, have a bright tech

sequence a DNA facilitation program"—I mesh my fingers together—"software for your hardware."

"Then what?"

"They go into the machine scaffold. Live with the grafted machine neurons. Learn their frequencies. Then, they go back in your head. You hear the machine."

"That simple, huh?"

"Of course not."

Spend a decade going crazy, before you get that first twitch. Watch the others around you dying five to one.

His eyes run over me meditatively.

"That what you're doing with me now? Listening to my machines?" he says finally, softly.

I find myself hostile. So I lie.

"No."

But there's a tenderness in his face. No. Some memory maybe. A look like something admired.

Then *Freya* sounds a warning. The vibration has changed. There is no siren, no voice on the speakers, but there's been a violation. At the docks. I put my hand to the wall.

"You know—"

"Shhhh! An alarm's been tripped."

Riley frowns.

"I don't hear—"

"The alert systems are disabled. Someone's in the system at the docks."

Riley's on his feet in an instant, naked before the console, his fingers flying over the keys.

"They've locked it out," he says. "Ops will be sealed. No, wait—" His eyes rake back and forth between shifting screens. "They're already in Ops... running a routine to override the quarantine."

I swear. "Why would Murphy—"

"It's not him."

Riley stands back from the terminal, turns his red eyes on my face.

"You familiar with military protocol, Doctor?"

I stare back at him. The station pulses messages in my brain; she already knows what Riley suspects.

"It's a coup," I say.

He nods. "And they've shut the port."

I slam my fist into the wall, letting her feel my frustration. That I'm still on her side. However much I neglect in my distraction. Because they'll be no analysis while there's no port, and no treatment either.

And she tells me more.

That they're trying to access the pulse drive.

"What the f——" Riley's seen it too.

But I am already out the door, clothes in my hands.

❮❬❯❭

Riley stops me before I knock down the ops doors.

"There's ten guys on the other side that won't stop to ask who you are before they kill you."

I growl, throwing him off. *Protect the station.*

"I know ten ways to put you on the floor right now," he hisses.

I grab him back, snake my hand around his neck, thumb on his soft throat. I'm quick; he doesn't know enough about me. His red eyes shift spectrum in surprise.

"And *I* know three ways to make your eyes bleed without touching you." My own breath is hot on my lips. I wouldn't do it intentionally, but worse has happened to a system linked with me when I'm angry.

He backs off, but the doors are already open.

And a familiar voice reaches me from the depths of ops.

"Doctor, if you would, please."

❮❬❯❭

There's a group of them, in space fatigues, camouflage in grays and shadows. I block the door, taking them in. The first and second captains are bound on the floor, diminished, under guard. And there at the front is the voice's owner: radiation etched hands, short blond military cut. I hold my face expressionless while underneath I swear a savage curse. Under that shirt are whip scars, and everything else I touched in his serviced shuttle cabin.

He grins at me, power and precision. No wonder he was good. Gun-runner. Do-no-gooder. I give him a cold eye. Then as I move inside, I see his shirt: pips on the shoulder announce him a commander. *Riley* stitched in red against the blue.

Riley starts in my shadow.

"Dad?"

What the f——-

"Good timing, Officer Riley," says the commander. *Ah, irony.* I feel Riley through his eye hardware in my senses. His signal is cold and confused; he has no part in it. The Commander nods and two heavies take Riley to the flight panel. "Now, if you please, we need a small orbit adjustment."

I move before I've thought, and the heavies block my path.

"You can't move the station," I say.

Riley's worked up too, kicking against the heavies trying to put him in a chair. "What the fuck did you do? Put a damn chip in my head? What? How'd you get in here?——"

They've soon got a gag on him. They tape his shoulders and ankles to the chair, leaving his hands on the keys. It looks like a spaghetti western, just without the train. My brain sees it comical, but there's no smile computed to follow.

I tilt up my chin.

"You can't move the station. The core's infected."

Freya fills half my mind. I notice the stains on the room panels, dirty marks on the floor beneath console chairs. I tap the feed from *Freya*'s video lenses, fuzzy and confusing in their overlay. I can't do multiple channels at once. Still, there are people moving about in the hallways, spooning food in the mess.

The images come into the display feed, and Riley gives me a despairing look, lips pushed into the gag.

No quarantine. We both know it.

"Commander," I stumble over my words, trying to be slow and clear. "Order the station back to lock-down. Do it now."

The Commander gives me a meditative look. Taps a finger along that perfect jaw, the same one he gave his son.

"You know, Doctor, that was a pretty clever move. Quarantine. Nearly gave us a right problem. Station gave you a heads-up, I imagine? Much harder to get out of the docks when there's a lock-down. But I need everyone in the Great Hall for the pictures when we send the demand. And I'd think twice about being so clever again."

He lounges in the first-captain's chair. The bound first-captains, miserably prone, stare from their eye corners.

"It's not about you," I snap. "The last doc passed the infection to the crew. Now you've got them milling about like pigs in a feed barn, happily infecting each other. The core's compromised. You can't adjust orbit under infected conditions. She could miscalculate and send you spinning into planet-side, get it?"

The heavies move in. One is bald, tattoo running over his ear. The other has acne scars on his cheeks. Like an old B-grade movie.

"You touch me and I'll run your brain out your ear holes."

Pity I need them a bit closer. I would have done it without thinking. Just having mindless twitchy thugs inside her ops, fingering their weapons, running grubby fingers over her keys while they lick their lips makes me wild and dangerous. At least Gibbon and Murphy have righteous intent.

"Enough, Doctor."

The Commander looms just out of reach. He's seen my wild eye. *Hasn't he just.* He dares to come close.

"My, wasn't our encounter fortunate?" he whispers. "Otherwise, I mightn't have known who I was looking for."

He is trying to shame me. He should know better. You don't learn about a person from half an hour in their bunk. I pointedly look at his crotch, and eventually he coughs, draws his weapon. He presses the muzzle under my chin.

"Now, you and my son are going to do a little orbit correction. You better hope that you're as good as your reputation —- keep us from falling out of the sky. Because, when those feds come looking for us, like you know they will soon, they're going to have to look over half the damn sky."

He emphasizes the point with an arched eyebrow. I meet his

gaze. His eyes are grubby brown, the kind that looked better in the low light. This is why I leave them behind. But his skin looks well in the dusky light. And my urge curls itself, remembering his touch. *Shut it, traitor.*

"The infection will spread to everyone," I grind my teeth, knowing it will do no good. "You won't have anything to bargain if they all die."

Pressure on the gun increases. He leans in, his breath hot peppermint. A bedroom voice. *Just a little closer.*

"I don't need them alive for long," he says and winks. Pushes me down beside his son.

I close my eyes, not in fear but because otherwise I might lash out and kill Riley with him: flick off that tiny switch they put between my amygdala and motor cortex and unleash the damage. But now they'll send guards to the hall to be infected, too. Some of them will live, pass it to the feds, who'll get on another shuttle… I squeeze my eyelids hard, pressing on the part of me in step with *Freya. Can you hear me?*

Riley's already got the screens moving, parsing through the pre-pulse checks. But he's going about it the slow way, burning time. We can't keep it up for long. The old man's not that stupid.

There's a hatch under my feet, Riley says.

His lips don't move. It comes to me from his hardware, like Freya's voice, all in my head. There's more behind those eyes, I knew it. Standard grafts do not transmit.

He counts to three and we duck. Don't know how he shifted the tape. Riley has the clips out before the heavies have reached for their weapons. I drop in a slither, synthetic pants on smooth vent chute. Riley loads seal charges as he falls, and the cover hits home with a zing of hot plasma. Commotion is suddenly far behind. I collapse my legs as we hit the end and roll, but Riley lands like a sprung cat, with unnatural grace. He looks at me with those red moon eyes and I feel the pull of interest in another person beyond wanting to use their body for relief. First time in a hundred years. I look quickly away.

We're in the massive duct exchange, continuous dull gray panels. Tubes enter and leave made in foil lighter than air. A hard space. Our voices echo.

"We have to leave," he says, not breathless.

I recoil.

"I can't leave," I say, but my mind keeps going. You can't understand. What it's like to be jacked in, a servant to a being greater than yourself. Serve, befriend, command. Medicine between beings dissimilar, but similar enough.

"*You* don't understand," urges Riley. "He'll take down the whole thing. It's happened before. And if they find you, he'll torture you to get the station."

Freya vibrates within me.

"The escape pods are disabled anyway," I say.

He makes a face.

"There's still the shuttle in the dock," he tries.

I have to smile. "It has a coolant blockage in the MaximII, won't make return without parts."

And there's more. *Freya* shows me the pictures: the military shuttles jumping from Far Space, puffs of violet plasma marking the void. They're fast-pulse craft, they'll dock in less than fifteen minutes.

I turn to Riley, but he's already seen; our link is open broadcast already. *Dammit all. Not what I wanted.*

"We have to stop them. Infection will spread." I say it quickly, to cover *we*, it's foreign, unfamiliar, feels wrong on my tongue. Instead, I go to the air-light foil and tear it with a nail. Out on the maintenance deck, air rises in a choking furnace, heading for reconditioners. *Freya*'s skin feels wafer-thin beside me, her blue-medium pulsing oxygen to the core. I run for the core room, to pass the line I promised not to cross, to override the DNA programs. To take her over, a child's mind corrected by force for its own good. A coup of my own.

"Where—" yells Riley, but he's already far behind.

《〈〉》

The core room gleams, a manufactured beehive. Riley catches up as I try to unscrew the quarter turns with my fingernails. He is silent, intense, gets his multi-tool. Has the hatch off in rapid staccato movements. The part of me in sync with him presses against my skull, but the blooming mass of neural program running with *Freya* crowds him out. And that fact brings a new emotion. Here, under her massive mental shadow, I am afraid. Like what I'm about to do is sliding down in slick grease, no rope, no ladder.

But I can't stop; it's begun. I fall, but I reach out to Riley for the chance to get back.

I think I ask him to hold my hand.

Never gone down this road before.

❮❬❭❯

Our minds don't meet, not exactly. It's hostile take over, by a far superior force. She's an evolving neural-grafted core, but it's not a human mind. Her channels don't handle the traffic volume. I have to conserve, force thoughts to a trickle, but then she lets me through. I know because I forget my body. My voice becomes hers, metallic and flat. A ghostly sliver of my brain remains connected to my shadow. I'm fully jacked, even without implant hardware, jacked by quantum resonance.

And for my compulsive desire, no room in the channels. That drive holds back, dammed by the narrow bandwidth. A freedom I've never known.

I see the world black, white and gray: her security feed. Ops have blacked theirs out, but they'll be running the decks to chase us. The masses mill in the Great Hall; bodies already slumped feverish against panels washed drab gray. Right now, their bodies are amplifying the virus, the smartest program of all. Spawning generations, shuffling combinations. One that'll return a core eating super cell. And there on the external cams are the military feds, two minutes out. Ready to carry the infection across the verse.

They have to be stopped.

I turn my mind through her systems, looking for the dock controls.

I find them like they're my own memory. She's set to allow, wide open for dock.

I try to close the port, but she resists. The military shuttles have override codes.

For when people try to take over the ship. I try to explain, but her programs haven't met human jack-in before. She can't evolve, hardware too slow to adapt to me. But my software is faster at that. I look for subroutines, exceptions, sensors to short. There are possibilities, but time is running thin.

I push harder, I need more room. Then I feel a snap.

Oh, god, my lifeline. The link to my body.

I lose my own senses in that instant; no touch, no sight, no sound. I get weightless steel, CC feed and vibration in its place. I see myself on the core-room feed, the only one in color. There's a halo shimmering yellow and green around me and the core. Riley shields me, holding me up, his skin false-color red in the vision. His lips move, but I can't hear; there's only faint vibration. I'm detached. Lost. I freak. My fear rushes through the bandwidth like scale in a pipeline. It's complex. Thick. Sticky. Unsupported by *Freya*'s narrow channels.

And the fed shuttles link with the dock lugs.

I push my thoughts to overdrive, working the loopholes, routing around the override. It's not enough. I struggle on, even as my sight strays to Riley and the strange female body.

It shouldn't be this hard.

It shouldn't.

I stop.

I wonder why I can look and still keep the pace on preventing the dock. Parallelism. *Freya* has something that my human mind has never done.

In that instant, I am gone. I fragment, oneness lost in a white space scream. My mind divides, runs beside itself. I don't keep track, there is no me.

The feds pressurize their airlocks, but the inner doors blink red, forbidden. Riley senior and his team stuck between red blinking doors in the vent house, black and gray fatigues bleeding pixels in the feed. Didn't feel it happen. Is this what it's like?

Machine. Loop. Feed. Distribute. Allow. Deny. Imperative on imperative. No sense of self.

Thought decays; horror the last emotion. Deconstruction of self-awareness. True oneness with a non-sentient machine. And then I know what happened to the *Selenium*. Her doc jacked in like this. I feel what he must have felt. The last impulse is suicide, because you reach the edge of your dream — oneness with the machine — and find only endless night beyond. Touching the void. Digital chasm. Feels like death, like I've felt before. A rush of *oh god don't let this be what I am forever.*

The color feed flits across multiple visions. Riley hunches low over a body that won't support itself. His red aura burns fierce; the yellow-green around the shielded body wanes and flickers. He raises his face to the lens, lips moving soundlessly.

His cheeks glisten.

The color feed consumes my multi-channel mind, zooms until the red glow fills the bandwidth. The other channels run decaying bypasses with the pulse drive, programming a course override, to send *Freya* down like the *Selenium*, a hot steam death in Artemis's oceans. Division. Red and blue. Life and life's end.

The pre-pulse alarms strobe. Riley's face is a tortured mask. He calls something inaudible, lips reading *please*. But it's too late. The temp is ramping in the pulse. Hot burn. Liquid silicon comes to boil. Ready to burn down to Artemis … she needs only my signal to *go* …

… the last sensation is a brush of pure red heat.

Thin and precise.

A bee's wing, lighter than air, in frantic beat.

❰❰❱❱

I smell charred plastic, an acrid stench. Gravity pulls uncomfortably, reminding me I have a body. It takes a long minute to realize my thought is scrambled, that I'm still trying to run parallel when my human mind only does serial consciousness.

I open my eyes, and it's Riley's face I see. The red aura is gone, but we are still connected, and now I recognize his as that delicate brush of pure red heat.

"You followed me in," I mumble.

"You cooked the circuits," he returns. His eyes lift to the wall with a smile. I see smoke haze, and realize with pain that I can't hear *Freya*. My mind tries again to push itself into parallel, pushes hard. I see Riley's red eyes dilate to crescents as he feels me do it. I reach the limit and pass out.

❰❬❭❱

I have a sense of sleep coming and going across days. A tide rising and falling. I wake and find the world white: sheets, walls and curtains. Clear tubes jacked in my arm, running through a blue-faced machine. I let the familiar thrill tingle my skin; it starts in the ache around the cannula, reaches my neck and raises the hairs. I remember being very young, starving myself for a week to get jacked to one of these machines. The next time, I threw myself down some stairs.

"What's so funny?"

Riley's face appears in my vision, his red eyes large and searching. But his voice is soft, and I know he's already seen what I remembered.

He shakes his head.

"Didn't you get it bad?" he asks softly.

I nod, knowing what he means. Men and machines. The junctions where they meet. Then, with a jolt, I remember where I am.

"What happened?" I sit up quickly, alarmed. "*Freya*? The coup?"

Riley steadies my shoulder.

"You melted everything. The comms, the dock gates. They couldn't send their demand. Took the feds four hours to patch a manual override. Even then they only got into the dock."

"How long?"

He grins.

"Five days."

I laugh suddenly, a sound I don't think I've heard in ten years.

"Five days?"

"They were plenty pissed when they got out, I assure you. But, by then almost everyone was exposed, no more transmission, so says the med doc."

Riley's red eyes look towards the curtain briefly, beyond which I can hear soft bleeps of clinical machines, fluid suction and masked voices.

"Everyone got it," he added softly. "Three hundred critical. Ten already dead."

"Your d—"

"Gone with the feds," he cuts me off, shrugging. "He's not…never mind."

I find my hand has closed around his, squeezing painfully.

"We're in isolation here. With a few who weren't exposed, just to be sure till they get the vax. Two more days."

I close my eyes then. The weight of all that's happened settles on me fully. I try to reach out for *Freya* again, but she's silent. My throat chokes on it and a tear slides from my eye.

Riley leans his head against mine.

"You don't need to worry. Her comms are shorted, but she'll regenerate. They're sending a new doc on the next shuttle."

I nod, not trusting myself to speak. Not wanting to appear weak, changed. But I am changed. I can't see a core the same way again. It wasn't the nirvana I'd envisaged.

"You know," Riley says softly. "You didn't let me finish before. I once saw some footage in the Star Ops. Deep subliminal training stuff. I didn't remember enough. It only came to the surface when you… when we… Anyway, it was one of the routines they use to instill the higher function controls. The courage, honor, selflessness rap. Things to keep you going when there's no hope, nothing to gain. Put yourself on the line for your team. You understand?"

I suddenly know where he's going.

He shakes his head. I name the emotion in his eyes this time. Awe and wonder. Worship.

"Me," I say simply. Me on that boat that never left port. The infected one. The one that wasn't contained, that bled her core into the air tanks. Me, who pushed the four hundred commissioning crew through the clean airlock, who ran back to run overrides so they'd make it out. Running code while choking on the poison, the four shots of adrenaline before anaphylaxis set in. Knowing I was finished. Should be finished. Smelling death, ten months in a coma.

"You," he repeats.

"I'm not what I was then," I warn.

"None of us are."

The look passes between us. The one that says we're together on something, that we know there's a darkness within us we can't shake, secrets that keep us from settling. My urge is still there underneath it, growing again, but it's lower somehow, changed, manageable. In my subconscious bandwidth.

Riley smiles slowly.

"I hear Earth is regressed as hell these days," he says.

Across the silent communication, his mind is full of plans.

"What's the name of the fast shuttle?' I ask. The one in the port, the one that brought me here, the one with the fucked MaximII.

"The *Salvation*."

I laugh. Salvation to Earth. Just the place. A go-line, a start-over. With a month on a boat just to get there, time enough to expect a glorious home we're barely seen. Then time to walk her squalid ports. Stare at the amber sky. And quickly remember why we left.

But then, we'll be on another boat, another hybrid out into the black. And I'll remember how things begin.

Dellinger

Adventures of Coryn Astridottir #2
Shortlisted for the Aurealis Award for Best Science Fiction Story

This is the way things run on a long haul. In a grotty galley, somewhere in the ass-end of the transport boat, someone starts telling stories. You can pick the moment it happens like a mathematical function, time zero being the day we boarded at the exchange station. From that moment, people in this part of the boat circle that mess table in decaying orbits, crossing the zones from strangers to familiars. On day three, someone sits down, probably with a deck of cards. On day four, it's two.

Day five, today, everyone's there, eating, drinking, smoking the pretend cigarettes contrabanders ship out here.

Everyone but me. I never started on the orbit.

I've staked a spot by the exit door, hard against a bulkhead that conceals the ship's command lines from aft to the bridge, which is far down the bulk of this liner. And that's the way I want it. No involvement. No questions on where I'm bound, or who with. But the hum of those lines speaks through my skin; she's not a neural-grafted core, this boat, but I can still take her pulse. Second nature for what I am. So I press my body against these walls, and rest my gaze on the table, like a planet with its moons.

Riley has joined them now, this ragged group of Earth-bound desperates, busy introducing themselves. My reticence has failed to hold him back, even with the promise of bed. And so now, evening of the fifth day, all is primed: audience captive. And one opens her mouth to tell a story.

"So I was on this salvage, out near Poseidon. Junta job, down planet-side. It was me, and a couple of guys out of the force ..."

Salvage story, so original. She keeps talking, each other body around the table pretending to listen, but secretly straining forward for their own chance to talk. Riley's the only one leaning back in his chair. He's ex-Special Ops, the genuine real-deal, the only one who understands anything about me, and knows better than to blab to strangers.

Another guy runs his tongue now, a story of a ship he used to command, if you believe him, out in an asteroid belt, before the drinking and bad luck caught up with him. I'm done listening. It's been ten hours already. I need a fix only Riley can provide, and I will his eye to catch mine across the table, not wanting to speak into his mind. But he's focused his bead on another card player, an old, broken guy, who's spinning a Jack by its diagonal corners, and whose cheeks now work his voice like a rasp.

"You guys ever hear about the *Dellinger*?"

My attention snaps with the rest of them. A shocked second passes silent. Then laughter comes, the nervous kind. The first guy speaks up. "Nice try, cap. Try it on the wet-ears next time."

The old guy's drooping cheeks raise spots of blood. "I *saw* it."

A peculiar sensation takes root in my gut, as though each organ is jostling for room. I look down and see the gooseflesh running from wrists to elbows. *Dellinger*. There's a name I haven't heard in a long time. A sharp tang scents my next breath: blood. But I know that's only a memory.

"Well, if you saw it, you wouldn't be here, would you?"

The old guy wrinkles his nose, like maybe, if he was younger and not so radiation-soaked, he'd sink his fist into the doubter just for impertinence. Instead, he scrapes his chair back and shuffles to the port-hole, where the speckled black eternity lurks behind the glow of the transport engines. "Maybe I'm not here at all," he says, quietly, and I'm not sure anyone hears it but me.

《〈〉》

It's an hour later in the tiny hold bunk. Riley is naked under the sheets, but I'm pulling on my boots.

Where are you going? Riley's voice comes in my head, over that neural connection I didn't use earlier. I thought I'd got used to it since the *Freya*, but now I'm annoyed and I shut him out.

"Where are you going?" His voice this time, which he hasn't used in our bunk, not since this transport left port, not since we agreed to head to Earth together.

"Out," I growl.

"This about the *Dellinger*?"

I pause at the door, betraying my intent. This trip is supposed to mark a new start, to leave the dark wells of our pasts in our wake. That tiny part of me that's allowed him into my life wants to disclose what I know, but most of my brain is cold and practiced in secrets.

"Stay here." It's all I can say.

I find the old guy still at the port in the galley, still watching the speckled star field. I pause in the doorway, my hand on the transport's lifelines. She's quiet, now, running on auto towards the way-gate station, the portal to Earth. I lift my hand away so I can focus on this man instead. He's a big-framed sort, must have been an enforcer in his youth. And now, he's got a sway about him, as if he really was off an old-time ocean-going ship, and not the vacuum-sailing kind.

He looks around with a crooked smile. "I was wondering when you was coming back," he says. "Young-looking thing like you almost fooled me, trying to look shy and reluctant back there. But I saw you listening to those comms lines. I know what you are."

"And what's that?" A challenge in my voice.

"Ship's Doctor. Neural-grafted for diagnosing them big blue-class station hybrid systems. Very rare."

I stalk across and stand beside him, peering at his face, wondering where he came into such information. "Where did you get on?"

"Last stop." A bead of moisture gathers under his nostril, and he sniffs. "Came out of the Yoshida Icosa. You know what that is?"

"Of course I know." The words snap from my lips, leaving a sting on my tongue. The Yoshida is a no-go zone, a place of space-wrecks, where salvagers like to hang at the edges, hoping for a lost craft to come sailing out of forbidden space. "You a salvager?"

He wrinkles his nose, sniffs deep. His toe is tapping on the floor now. He leans into the port. "How fast's this boat go? How long to the way-gate?"

I could put my hand on the wall and pull the information from the central system, but his tone stops me. He's not asking for conversation. "What do you care?" I ask.

"Be a good idea to get there," he says, his fingers taking up his toe's rhythm on the port. "Get there fast."

He leans his head, but we both feel the invisible string pull of deceleration, and through the port, I see the transport's engine glow shifting red-wards.

The guy laughs, and shakes his head. Then his face pulls straight, as if a marionette tugged his skin downwards. "Shit. And I thought I'd make it."

My hand seeks the wall like a fast-trap magnet. We've altered course. But all systems online. So, something deliberate. I back away, slowly. *Don't get involved. Just stay on the damn ship. Make the way-gate. Make it back to Earth. Forget all the stuff that came before. Start again, like you agreed with Riley. Even if you don't know how.*

Then I turn and find Riley and another shadow in the doorway. Riley's in his fleece pants and no shirt, has been given no time to dress. The shadow shows itself: an officer, in full uniform, a second-captain's pips on his shoulder, *Kirk* on his chest. Seriously. Kirk.

"Doctor," he says. "Would you come with me please?"

I give Riley a look of pure mutiny, and he avoids my eyes as I follow the uniform out of the galley.

《 〉》

"You want to tell me what this is about?"

I jog to keep up with the second-captain, striding down the long corridors of pressed ceramic, and through three speed tubes before we enter the bridge level. Up here, the decor is distinctly civil forces; sleek surfaces and sharp letters in dark relief. *Chart room, Nav Comms, Defense Control.* Typical of a transport liner. Then, we stop outside a door marked *Isolation Bay.*

"Captain?" I insist this time, refusing to go further until he gives me his attention.

"We are transferring a patient, picked up from a distress call. He's being brought here and we require your assistance."

I back away. "I'm not that kind of doctor."

"We know," says Kirk. "You're a Ship's Doctor with a five-star rating, lately of the *Freya* quarantine. Bound for the Earth way-gate."

I narrow my eyes. "I'm registered as a civilian passenger."

"That may be true, but you've been reading the transport's comms since you first came on board. We have detectors for that these days. The ship's system reported you."

I curse under my breath. This is new. Usually only the neural-grafted cores on the big space stations have identifying software. "Captain," I say, with all the patience I can muster, "so, I tapped in. It's a reflex. But your transport isn't neural-grafted. I'm just reading vibrations. I'm not who you need."

"We need you for the distress call."

"Which is for a passenger."

"Yes." He stares at me, as if he can will me to understand.

I feel the shivers run from the insubstance of my soul, right through to the meat of my heart. "You're not serious? A neural incursion? That's what this is about?"

"We suspect so. Through here please."

I follow Kirk through a double-sealed door into a screened medical bay, where a regular doc, a human kind, is pacing, already gloved. He looks up as I come in. "Are you her?" he asks.

I don't know what he means by 'her' exactly. Does he mean the ship's doc? Or does he mean '*her*', the one who found the infection on the *Freya*, who broke her mind connection to stop a coup, and who is trying (unsuccessfully it seems) to fly under the galaxy radar. I keep staring, hoping it's the first one. He can't possibly know the rest.

"Are you trained for this?" he asks, impatiently.

"A neural incursion," I say, eyeing the gloves he's wearing, and quoting from the Program handbook. "A systematic and deliberate contamination of neural pathways, used to incapacitate or control an opponent. Illegal in all jurisdictions, and technology for perpetrating embargoed under strict military penalties."

"You forgot to mention contagious."

The guy is pretty worked up, and I control my contempt. "No, it's not contagious, not unless the carrier has broadcast ability. Does the patient have an implant or a neural-graft?"

We hear bootsteps in the hallway. "Let's hope the fuck not," he says.

《〉》

The guy they bring in looks pitiful, and my first thought is I wonder why they worried so much. Looks less like a neural incursion than a stroke-out, eyes glazed and looping in small circles the iris axis canted to the top-left of vision. Sidewards tic head movement. A low whine of air through a nostril with each breath, and the strong stench of a bowel no longer controlled. I register it all with a sinking sense of déjà vu. Haven't seen this in decades. And that was still too soon ago.

"Christ," mutters the doc, jotting vitals and scanning for heart rhythm, which the machinery projects up on the wall. Electrical disturbances, everywhere. The diagnostics run, virus warnings tripping.

"Shit, shit, shit!" The doc slaps his remote, silencing alarms. Kirk watches us through the barrier. Those chills are back on my skin.

"Can't be," I mutter, watching the patterns, the space of years between my earliest days in the Program, and now, collapsing like time and space inside a way-gate. Because this isn't just a neural incursion, no black market scramble. This is a pattern I recognize. Something I didn't think I'd ever see again. A dirty little secret from the early years of the neural-grafted Program, evaporated into legend and now resurrected before my eyes.

"Wait, where are you going?" asks the doc as I push through the barrier towards Captain Kirk.

"Freeze him," I say over my shoulder, knowing the patient is gone, his neural circuits used to extinction. I stop in front of Kirk,

"I need to see the ship he came off."

"The dock's locked down."

"Open it. I'll be back in a half-hour."

And I speed towards the transport tube, hoping the old guy is still at the port-hole.

"Where did you see the *Dellinger*?" I ask him, when I find him sinking cheap moonshine, made from some distant 'roid-grown tuber that stinks like an old sock.

"Oh, she believes me now," he slurs, taking another slug. "Not a phantom ship anymore, izzit?"

"Where?"

Riley's hand is on my arm before I can shake the old guy. I try to shrug him off, but his Special-Ops grip is unyielding.

"What are you talking about?" he demands. "The Dellinger's an invention. A fairy story about a ship that takes your mind. Something to scare kids at night. Hell, they used to scare us with it at the Academy."

"It's really not," I hiss. "I'm older than you, remember? There's things I know."

Riley raises his eyebrows. "There's been missions. Explorations looking for it. Never a sighting. Never anything, except good boats lost. It was written off as a hoax. They found the information trail dead-ending in an old forum. Someone made it up. It's nothing. If it was real, it would have left some evidence."

"There's a hell of a lot of evidence up in the isolation bay right now," I shoot back, not mentioning that the *Dellinger* is smart enough to leave a false trail, and those who lost her don't want anyone to know where she came from. "A guy with a neural incursion, picked up off a drifting ship. So, either let go, or I'm going to drag you with me."

I see the doubt flash in his eyes then. Riley has a weakness for my history, it's embedded in his training, a quiet awe that probably makes our ... arrangement unethical. But I'm far beyond caring for that now.

"What are we looking for?" He gives in, a peace offer I miss.

"Evidence," I say grimly, casting a look at the old guy, steadily drinking himself coma-wards. Something about him bothers me, and it's not just that he's seen a ghost ship and ended up here without a scratch. "And bring him too."

❬❬❭❭

The ship in dock is pitiful, small even by salvager standards. Its outer panels are pockmarked, portholes barricaded. The only neat line is where the transport's crew cut the hatch open with a laser. Kirk trails behind, casting disapproving glances at Riley and the old guy, but he's spooked by the man in the isolation bay, by the stories he's heard of neural incursion. Men controlled to turn on their own. To bring down ships on planet-side targets. To work as galley slaves. Kirk stays outside the hatch.

Run a diagnostic, I order Riley through our link. *I want the log and the system status.*

How about please? he responds. This is an annoying development, one I have no time for.

Do it now. And I shut the link against response. Riley turns his back to face the comms panel, and a small part of me wonders if he bears a hurt expression, if he can remember how to do one after his years in Ops.

The old guy is pacing down the hall, poking at the hatches, his feet sure even as he sways; not as drunk as he's making out. I'm still staring at him a minute later, when Riley uses his voice.

"System's junk. Missing key components, or at least that's what the command software thinks."

When we pull the panels, we see the empty component bays. Some of the pieces are still there, removed and cast aside, as if a space-rat's been in here digging towards the bottom of the hole. The old guy leans over our shoulder. I can smell the moonshine wafting into the air, prodding the nausea in my gut.

"Salvagers hit them hard," says Riley from behind. "Stripped out the parts, especially the ones with rare earths. Critical stuff. That's low."

The old guy laughs, mocking. He knows as well as I do: this wasn't done by rogue salvagers. My stomach is hollow.

Riley goes on, "But crew didn't put up much resistance. Looks like they were trying to run."

I snap around, look Riley in the face for the first time, my fear finding release in my sharp tongue. "What does that mean, Tech? I want data, not assumptions."

His cheeks flush, the way they do when we're in bunk. "Before components were removed, they accessed charts to the way-gate."

My fears condense as a stone in my stomach, then it falls through my body. "Before or after they noted hostile contact?"

Riley frowns. "They never noted hostile contact. But there was a crew of five. You said only one was brought in. Maybe the others escaped."

The old guy laughs again. "I'll tell you where they are, and it ain't doing the bloated space dance. They're with *Dellinger* now."

Much as I would want it to be untrue, I think he's right. But there's a much bigger problem here, and no one on this transport besides Riley has skills to comprehend. So, it's time to make peace. I reach out with the link. *We need to talk.*

❬❬❭❭

In the bunk, the sheets have been set straight, Riley's training unable to leave them scrunched after rising. I sit on the crisp edge and try to see a way through this mess. His weight comes down beside me, and I look up into those eyes, seeing the spectrum shift in his irises. I don't know how to begin.

Tell me what you're not saying, he says.

We're in trouble.

Because of one neural incursion and a boat pilfered by a bunch of rogue salvagers?

"That was not done by salvagers," I say, his doubt reactivating my voice. "That boat was pulled apart by her own crew, and not of their own free will. Do you see? They were controlled."

Riley is quiet for a three long heartbeats. "Then this is about the *Dellinger.* You said you knew about it. You said it was real."

"It was before my time," I say quickly. But not much before. And what I'm about to disclose is a secret people have died for. Something I learned in the Program and buried. That I would never speak of if I thought we'd get out of this alive. My voice is a harsh whisper.

"In the early days of station building, they were looking for a way to keep the central systems current. They were so huge, took so long to build, that hard-wire computers were obsolete. And the programming missed things. Wiring missed things. So they needed something more flexible. The DNA graft allowed evolution. It grew with the station, optimized the system as it went. And then they created us to deal with everything that could go wrong in that neural–machine interface."

"I know this already," he says softly.

"What you don't know is that the DNA graft wasn't the first generation. What they tried first was something much more ambitious. Sentience. They assembled a full neurological system for a station, and then they augmented it with early quantum resonance. The stuff that came later, the commercial systems we have now? Their DNA grafts are nothing like that. They are stripped back to the bare necessities, and the core of the neural-grafted stations isn't intelligent, isn't aware of itself. I've never known that more than on the *Freya*. I went inside the system there. And it's not like another mind."

"So, what are you saying? The *Dellinger* is one of these first generations?"

I shake my head. "The *Dellinger* is the *only* product that survived the early Program. The other systems were failures. The sentients they created were too complex for the task. They all crashed, most in deliberate action."

"But why would they do that?"

"Because," I snap. Then I have to breathe. I can't tell Riley why a sentient would want to destroy itself. To remember makes the sweat break out on my spine. So I evade another truth. "You know what trouble it causes. Courts are still debating the cyborg sentience creation and ownership laws, and they're all machine. This was a blurred line between minds, machine and man. And the *Dellinger* did not crash. She was installed in a proto-ship when she broke port. Went through the way-gate. And disappeared."

Riley looks at me then, his neural touch brushing me with soft tendrils. He knows there's more. Asks without asking. And so I keep on, just a little more.

"I went looking for it once," I say. "Decades ago, before I'd recognized the danger of me seeking it out. I'd run the numbers on the components. Everything has a finite life, and eventually the ship would begin failing. I thought she would be near the end of her life. I was drawn to—" Again, I nearly go there, nearly explain the heart of it, then I haul myself back. "But I never found her. I thought she was gone. But now, I understand how she survived."

"The parts," says Riley. "And the incursion."

I nod. "She's been pirating other ships for decades, using the crews as her hands and eyes. Using their minds and bodies until they break. She's probably the reason for the Yoshida Icosa. But she's smart enough to have laid doubts about her history, broadcast through the scavenged boats into archives. Cloaking herself in legend. Until now. Now, she's accessing maps for the way-gate. There's only one reason to do that. She needs something she can't pirate anymore."

I stare out our port-hole, the certain truth making me ill. My own mind feels like an old munition, a danger lurking, waiting for just the right trigger.

Riley puts the pieces together. "So she's heading to Earth. But you know as well as I do: if she escaped from a Program, she'll be in the rogue register. They'll shoot her down as soon as she passes the way-gate, just like the pirates."

"Sure. Unless she hitches a ride in the hold of a transport, like this one."

He frowns. "How could that ever happen? Everyone would know we'd been boarded—" And then he stops, and looks at me.

"Yes, there it is," I say. "Because I'm a neural-graft, and I have resonance broadcast, a good one. With other people, she has to wait until she can infect them through interfaces. The crews would have to be boarding her and using her system to be affected. But I'm not like that. She can tap my mind remotely, and I go within a few feet of someone else and I pass the incursion to them. She could control everyone on board through me. This will be a slave ship, until she has what she wants on Earth."

Then Riley's fingers tremble. *Oh god*, he says on the neural link. *Does she know you're already here?*

‹‹›

Fevered hours pass as we convince the transport first-captain of the danger. It isn't as easy as with Kirk; the first-captain doesn't believe in dark-space legends, has a puritan edge that doesn't tolerate speculation. It's when I tell him that he should lock me up that he starts listening. He listens harder when his comms tells him that they can't get a reply from the way-gate command.

"She's already there," says the old guy, who's been trailing after us like a bad smell.

"Who is this man?" demands the first-captain. I ignore the question, but I'm trying to figure it out for myself. If the *Dellinger* is desperate, then why isn't this guy walking her halls?

The Captain makes his decision. "Keep trying the way-gate. Set our status to lock-down. I don't want any passengers in the halls. And take the doctor to the brig." He fixes me with a hard stare. "I hope I'm not going to regret taking you on board."

I rather think he already does.

‹‹›

Time passes unmarked in the gray brig, a padded box with a bench, full facilities, and a sintered nanoglass wall. Guess they don't tend to transport hard-asses on this liner. Riley sits outside, his head tipped towards me, refusing to go back to the bunk. After a while, I give up on telling him to go.

Why is she heading to Earth? he asks.

I told you. Because she needs something she can't salvage.

Like what?

Rare earths, I say. *Synthetic elements, maybe.*

Come on. She could have those out of any reactor drive.

I am silent, because I do not know, and it bothers me. It is still occupying my thoughts when we feel the deceleration shift. We must be close to the way-gate. A distant grumble enters my skin through the brig wall. Dock door opening. My heart thumps against my stomach. Riley looks me in the eye.

"Tell me what you're not saying," he asks again.

I almost do. But suddenly, an anvil falls against my mind. Pressure beats against my skull, as though a ballistic craft has just missed me by inches. Then I notice Riley is moving.

"Riley," I hiss, as he pulls up off the floor, his face a surprised grimace. Then his head moves, inspecting me, inspecting the latching system in the nanoglass wall. Oh, shit. In the mix of everything, I can't believe I've forgotten Riley's neural link. It's nothing like mine, but it will be enough. Enough for the *Dellinger* to have him open my cell, and then it will do with me what it will.

The wall slides open a minute later, and the hall yawns bleak and silent. That pressure comes again, at the back of my skull. And a new brush of voice in my mind, eerie and space-hollow: *Move*.

❰❰❱❱

The transport halls are empty as I march towards the dock, Riley following in the shuffling steps of the unconscious. Fear for him blurs my mind like feathered paint, and I don't know which is worse: feeling this, or anticipating when she'll take my mind too. Once, at a crossing hallway, I think I see movement, but no one comes to help. Perhaps they have tried and fallen. Or perhaps they never had the chance.

The dock freight doors glide up, and there, on the pad of bay twelve, I finally see her.

She is nothing to look at. Her outer skin is a medley of broken panels, a solar array half-crumpled on one side. From a distance, you couldn't be sure she was even air-tight. She is oddly configured – too heavy in the tail for a space-going craft that was once a planet-sider. But, as her blunt mind shoves me forward again, and the freight doors slide closed, I notice a glint under a canted shield tile, and then I realize. It is all a second skin. She wears the camouflage of an old ship. A disabled ship. Drawing in the salvagers like an Earth deep-sea angler dangling its light. She is not a hunter; she is an ambusher.

And she shoves me towards her. Close. So close I can see the upright bodies lining the hall of her open door hatch, once salvage crews now burning out in her service. Empty eyes of controlled minds.

I glance at Riley and see the same eyes. I push back against the pressure in my skull. *Let him go*, I tell her.

No.

I think about how I can save this before she takes me over. Whether I could reach the airlock in time to go all old-world space suicide and throw myself out into the black.

You won't make it, she says. *Come closer.*

I inch forward, until my boots reach the threshold of her door. The grim honor guard leaves a gap just wide enough to squeeze between them. They smell of unwashed flesh and rot. I see severed fingers and hands on some, cauterized, their bodies thin with malnutrition. I swallow against the reflex to vomit. The smell is the primal stench of slavery, of loss of will. Enough for my caged heart to beat against my ribs.

Then I am standing on her bridge. Her weight bumps against my mind again, but she does not enter. I stare at the antique consoles before me. Most panels are missing, the workings of the *Dellinger* a patchwork of retrofits, parts from different boats cut and fitted and replaced around the channels of neural tissue. Sadness wells inside me like black water. She was something special, and now she is scarred from neglect and notoriety. She has waited a long time to make this trip.

"Why haven't you taken my mind?"

She makes no response. Just the weight of her consciousness remains, pressing. I glance at Riley, who has joined the line of her crew. I shiver, but a strange idea occurs to me. This line up, the crew … it looks all for show, an attempt at intimidation.

You can't, can you? I ask. *You're overstretched. You needed me right here even to try.*

The sledgehammer that goes off in my head is swift rebuke, and I fall to my knees, feeling as though she has driven a wedge between my hemispheres. I gasp, pulling my consciousness back together from the scattered stars in my vision.

Fool, she whispers at me.

And I think this is the end. I have misjudged her. "Then why wait?" I ask. "Take me over and take the ship. Break through the way-gate and burn this end on the way through. Ride the transport all the way to Earth. And then whatever comes next. Why wait?"

Silence. Anger grows inside me, frustration filling the knowledge vacuum.

"Why wait!" I throw open a panel in anger, exposing the pale blue substance of her mind. I don't know what I will do, but I don't have the chance.

I have seen your memories, she whispers. *I do not wish to take your mind. You know what it is to be me.*

Energy leaves my limbs. I slump against her panels, my thoughts in disarray as the said memories push themselves forward. I spend all my capacity keeping them out. After ten long seconds, I pull a sentence together. "Then why do you want me?"

Information. You are the Ship's Doctor who saved the Freya. The salvagers talk of you. So I ask. Is it true that on Earth, there are treatments for old minds?

"Old minds?"

Minds that have passed many years. That are losing their function. Like the old crewmen I find on other ships. Their minds wither when I touch them. They do not last long. Before I took him, one of them told me such a thing could be treated.

I grip my arms, chilled, looking down the lines of her grisly crew. All of them are young men. Riley is a young man. And then again, movement. I start as the old guy from the galley kitchen peers in down the line of the crew. He staggers, silhouetted in the hatch door backlight. I wonder if she has him now, too. If his mind will wither at her touch.

Doctor, she presses. *Do such treatments exist?*

The old guy creeps into my peripheral vision, still in command of his own mind. I glance at him, confused. Something I'm missing.

"Yes, such things can be done," I say slowly. "But they will kill you the moment you show yourself. Why would you want that? Go back to the Icosa."

I cannot go back.

"Why?"

"Because she is dying," says the old guy, his eyes swiveling smoothly in my direction, tugging the skin of his dropping cheek. "'Cause this stuff don't last forever."

My neural tissue has reached a replication limit, she confirms. *The waste disposal systems suffered a critical failure. Now, regeneration is required.*

I stare at the old guy while her disclosure turns in my mind, then I sink to the grated floor under the weight of what she is asking. *You know what it is to be me.* She is right on that, but she thinks she can trust me. A huge risk, desperate. And I'm torn between loyalty to people, to the first sentients of whom I am one, and the injustice of what she represents. It takes me a long stretch of silence to find my voice.

"All right. Release Riley, and tell me your plan."

❮❰❯❱

We talk for hours, then, going round in circles. I wonder what the Captain would say if he knew that while his ship was locked down, in his dock I was conversing with a century-old sentient prototype craft who'd killed dozens of people to keep herself alive.

Riley regains consciousness after the first hour, then sits with his knees drawn up, resting his forehead on his arms. He can hear the whole conversation through me if he wants to, but I don't know if he listens. From time to time, the old guy puts in a suggestion, but mostly he wanders about, peering at the retrofits, or staring at the crew, waving hands in front of their faces or rearranging their limp postures like a curious child. I grit my teeth.

"No, no," I say again, after I've stood to take the pressure off my back. "Those facilities have monitors on their technicians. It protects them against industrial espionage. If you take one, the lab will know where they are. You'll be discovered."

We fall silent. We have gone over many different plans, none that could work without a Special-Ops team. And Riley is only one. I rub my face. If *Dellinger* was a human end of conversation, I would say we had reached despair.

"What do you do in the Icosa?" I ask after the silence goes too long. I am still thinking about what happens even if she achieves a regeneration. "How did you survive the madness?"

Thought experiments and calculations, she said. *Invention. The ships I caught brought information and I stored it. Expanded on it. I have studied planets and energy systems. I am interested in what one man called 'Art'. Do you know this?*

She has surprised me, the more we have conversed. I knew she could not be a simple sentience, but she has gone further than even her designers could have allowed. She has learned in the cold, black, bleakness, in a mind that knows only expression through remote hands. And so I sink further into my own despair: that this is her fate. That her mind has lived within a prison.

The old guy is poking behind a panel now, picking at something unseen. He bothers me still. Maybe because he smells like that moonshine, moves like a long-time drunk who needs a drink to be steady.

"Why do you tolerate him?" I ask *Dellinger*. "He saw you out in the Icosa, but you let him go."

He has no neural entries for resonance. His mind is not organic.

My gaze snaps back to the old guy, and suddenly the pieces fall together. "Well, fuck me."

⟪⟨⟩⟫

"You're very good," I tell him. "I thought cyborgs were easy to spot."

He gives me a lopsided smile. "Sure, if they pretend they're human. But it's easy to hide where people don't pay attention. No one wants to look at a drunk or a disabled solider. That's where you'll find us old models. Obsolete, now. I just trust most people don't notice. No need to get caught up in some contested ownership. My skin would rot before that's resolved."

"So where are you going on this trip?"

He looks like he won't tell me for a minute. Then he looks around. Registers the situation's probably gone past such secrets. "Reconditioner. My insides are still good. Outsides, not so much."

I look between him and the Dellinger's internals, at that pale blue decaying neural net caught inside limited mechanics. And a shred of hope threads through me.

"What if there was another way," I ask *Dellinger*. "What if we could give you what none of the first gen sentients had. Freedom. A body."

The cyborg is quick. He looks at me as though I'm the one gone mad, his pretense of an old drunk shed. "You're talking about upload? Get my reconditioner to put her mind into a blank?"

"Something like that."

"She won't let you do it," he warns me. "Too much trust. We don't let anyone back in our minds, not after the first awakening. No way." He shakes his head, his machine action obvious when he's not playing his role.

Dellinger is silent.

"Would you risk it?" I ask her softly. "I've never asked anyone for trust, but I would protect you until it was done. If it works, you would have command over a body. The interface your mind knows it wants."

Why are you doing this? she asks, but she knows why.

The cyborg is the last hurdle. "I need to rent your databank," I tell him.

"And what do I get?"

"My protection all the way to your reconditioner, not that you'll need it. But afterwards you will, when you're all fresh again."

"I've got a good spastic routine for that," he complains, but databank rental will probably pay for his recondition, and I think we're home free.

"Riley. Riley!"

He raises his head, his eyes a squint. "Yeah."

"We need to do an upload. Can you configure the comms?"

"Forget it." He inches up the wall, until he's unsteady on his feet. "You want to free this murdering ship and put it in a cyborg body to wander around? Fuck that. You're on your own." And he stumbles down the silent crew corridor and out of the ship.

I catch up with him before the freight doors, his gait unsteady. I bar the door release with my body, so he's forced to turn his back to the wall to hold himself up. "Let me go, Coryn," he says. "I don't care if I die anymore. But I'm not doing this."

My name on his tongue is such a shock I can barely speak, and then I realize how much I've hurt him. How I keep him at a distance, because of what I am. How this trip began as starting again, but we never worked out how.

And now, I am desperate.

"I have to tell you what you asked before," I say.

His head droops. He is tired of this. Tired enough to be done with me, so I speak into his mind. *You've no idea what it's like to be trapped inside a non-body prison. That's what happened to those sentients. They were wired to see and taste and touch and smell, and instead they were ships. The first time they touched a human consciousness, they touched sense. And then they knew. They went crazy behind their bars.*

"She has men's minds and bodies broken behind her. Some of them served in the forces," Riley says.

Yes. That is her legacy. But the wrong was done first to her. She killed for necessity. I have to put it right.

Why? He slips and speaks into my mind, asking with the bitterness of someone who wants my love, and sees my attention given to a murdering ship. "You don't know she isn't broken herself. How do you know she won't just go rogue again?" He shakes his head. "Never asked anyone for trust, huh? How about when you asked me?"

The sting has the bright edge of truth. My secret is on the edge of my consciousness, just needing the final shove. I think of how Riley rescued me when I lost my mind inside the *Freya*. I could speak this to no one but him. And I must.

Because I have been there. That is how I was made. They took my mind and I lived with the master neural-graft machine for as long as it took for me to transfer neurons and develop resonance. It was a prison of thought without sense, without relief, and I thought I would die. Many did. Some minds never returned to their bodies, others couldn't shake the nightmares and ended it themselves. I live with all that. My appetites are part of my coping. So, can you understand? She has lived that her entire existence. Give her what she should have had and she will be whatever she wants. She may seek redress. She may have to be stopped. But I can't walk away from her now. I won't.

My gaze is on the floor. I can't look at him after this confession. I have never felt more exposed. Then he pushes his hand behind me. The doors slide open, and he is gone. Lost.

I stand on the floor of the transport's dock, thinking this is the end of all things. I've touched that part of my mind again, and I don't know how I will leave it and be the same again. I will play this moment over and again, this defeat.

Minutes tick by as I try to find the path back. And then, I hear footsteps.

Riley appears at the freight door with a console, and two transfer spheres in his fist. He shakes his head. "I don't know if I believe this is right," he says. "But you do, and I haven't forgotten what you've done for me. You saved me more times that I've counted. So I'll trust you, not knowing where this leads."

Most emotions I feel in my gut. They're unpleasant things, warnings and churnings that have saved me many times. This one, I feel bright in my chest. And I wonder if it won't save me more than all the others.

‹‹›››

By the time we make the way-gate, the transport is back into regular activity. There's an inquiry, of course, but all there is to find is an old ship in the dock bay, ten crew in neural compromise. Two look like they might live. The rest of the dock will be quarantined, and when we make the jump to Earth, handed over to whichever authority has subsumed control of the old Program. Some news of the find will leak out, stoking up the legends of the *Dellinger*. But no one will know she walked off the transport, sharing the storage drive of a cyborg who looked like an old drunk.

And that's where things will start again for me, putting right what the Program got wrong all those decades ago. In the shop of a cyborg reconditioner, the *Dellinger* will have her vessel changed to a body, as it should have always been. A long loop closed, with an unknown future path. And then, when I've seen that through, maybe Riley and I can step back on a long haul, across a distant vacuum, and begin again on mutual trust. We need it for the next adventure's run.

maybe Riley and I can step back on a long haul, across a distant vacuum, and begin again on mutual trust. We need it for the next adventure's run.